# DEEP SPACE
# CREW BOOK

James Van Hise

# PIONEER BOOKS

# Recently Released Pioneer Books. . .

MTV: MUSIC YOU CAN SEE                                                    ISBN#1-55698-355-7

TREK: THE NEXT GENERATION CREW BOOK    ISBN#1-55698-363-8

TREK: THE PRINTED ADVENTURES             ISBN#1-55698-365-5

THE CLASSIC TREK CREW BOOK               ISBN#1-55698-368-9

TREK VS THE NEXT GENERATION            ISBN#1-55698-370-0

TREK: THE NEXT GENERATION TRIBUTE BOOK  ISBN#1-55698-366-2

THE HOLLYWOOD CELEBRITY DEATH BOOK    ISBN#1-55698-369-7

LET'S TALK: AMERICA'S FAVORITE TV TALK SHOW HOSTS  ISBN#1-55698-364-6

HOT-BLOODED DINOSAUR MOVIES           ISBN#1-55698~365-4

BONANZA: THE UNOFFICIAL STORY OF THE PONDEROSA  ISBN#1-55698-359-X

# Exciting new titles soon to be released

THE KUNG FU BOOK                                    ISBN#1-55698-328-X

TREK: THE DEEP SPACE CELEBRATION       ISBN#1-55698 330-1

TREK: THE DEEP SPACE CREW BOOK        ISBN#1-55698-335-2

MARRIAGE & DIVORCE -HOLLYWOOD STYLE  ISBN#1-55698-333-6

TREK: THE ENCYCLOPEDIA                  ISBN#1-55698-331-X

THE LITTLE HOUSE COMPANION          ISBN#1-55698~332-8

**PUBLISHER: Hal Schuster**     **DESIGNER: Ben Long**     **EDITOR: Chuck Sperry**

Library of Congress Cataloging-in-Publication Data
James Van Hise, 1959—

    Deep Space Crew Book

      1. Deep Space Crew (television, popular culture)
  I. Title

Published by Pioneer Books, Inc., 5715 N. Balsam Rd., Las Vegas, NV, 89130.

First Printing, 1994

# Table of Contents

# Deep Space Nine Crew Book

*On November 13, 1993 the Universal Studios amphitheater in Studio City, California, featured the first ever public gathering of the entire crew of Deep Space Nine. The only other time the crew of the STAR TREK spin-off had gathered together before the public was in 1992 at a private invitational press conference at Paramount Studios. But this time the fans would be able to meet the stars in person.*

# MEET THE CAST OF DEEP SPACE NINE

Referred to as "Universal Studios: Hollywood," the original Universal Studios tour is constantly adding attractions and special events to draw visitors. Such was the case on November 13, 1993. The air was thick with tension and excitement as the audience filled the amphitheater. These people had come for the rare opportunity to get an intimate look at the cast of one of the most popular and inventive shows ever aired.

Finally, a representative of Universal Studios walked on stage, made a brief introduction and exclaimed, "Ladies and gentlemen put your hands together for the cast of DEEP SPACE NINE!" The audience of several hundred people erupted into applause as all of the actors came out on stage. The moderator introduced each cast member:

"She started her career as a tap dancer on Broadway and now she plays Major Kira. Welcome Nana Visitor!"

"A New Jersey native, he has enjoyed a successful career in TV with recurring roles in BEAUTY AND THE BEAST, BROOKLYN BRIDGE and many other guest-starring roles. Please welcome Ferengi entrepreneur, Quark—Armin Shimerman!

"Born and raised in Dublin, Ireland, he continues his role as Miles O'Brien from THE NEXT GENERATION, please welcome Colm Meaney!

The Deep Space Nine cast at Universal Studios, Hollywood. November, 1993

Photo c 1994 Alvert L. Ortega

"The youngest regular cast member of any STAR TREK series, but no newcomer to acting, this basketball-playing, bike-riding young actor plays Jake, the son of Commander Sisko. Let's put your hands together for Cirroc Lofton.

"Beginning her career as an elite model, she is now Lieutenant Jadzia Dax, Starfleet Science Officer. Let's hear it for Terry Farrell!

"This actor came straight from England about a year ago to begin filming STAR TREK DEEP SPACE NINE, leaving behind a career in theatre and television to play the role of Dr. Julian Bashir. Please welcome Siddig El Fadil!

"A Tony Award-winning stage actor who has also made his mark in feature films and television, best known for his six-year- portrayal of Chief of Staff Clayton Endicott the third in the hit TV series BENSON, please welcome Security Chief Odo, Rene Auberjonois!

"Finally, a long respected stage actor, jazz musician and professor of theater, best known for his television role on A MAN CALLED HAWK and SPENSER FOR HIRE, currently Starfleet Commander in charge of Deep Space Nine, Benjamin Sisko, please welcome Avery Brooks!"

For the first time since the inception of Deep Space Nine, the entire cast was assembled in public.

## A Man Called Brooks

The moderator began his discussion with Avery Brooks, probably the most press shy members of the cast. In fact, Avery's only major interview appeared in *TV Guide* a year after Deep Space Nine premiered. The moderator asked what it was like to move from SPENCER FOR HIRE into his own series, A MAN CALLED HAWK, and if there was a lot of pressure involved in starring in a series. Avery replied, "There was a lot of pressure, but at the same time I was able to make more of my own mistakes by myself. Television is done by committee: the more control you have, the better. So I enjoyed it thoroughly."

A young boy in the audience asked what the actors liked best about working on DEEP SPACE NINE. "Actually, what I enjoy most is coming to work with all these people," Avery stated, with a sweeping gesture that encompassed his fellow performers. "It's true!"

The other performers answered the boy's question. Rene made a sour expression and said in an exaggerated voice, "I like doing the makeup for two hours! That's my favorite part of the day!"

Siddig added, "I like the variety best of all. Every day is something different. Going somewhere else. Getting lost somewhere else. Getting found somewhere else."

Said Terry, "I'd have to agree with Avery," affirm-

Avery Brooks at Universal Studios Hollywood, November, 1993.

**Photo c 1994 Alvert L. Ortega**

ing the pleasure of working with this particular ensemble of performers.

Cirric Lofton simply stated, "I like everything."

## Hours of Overtime

Colm Meaney suddenly found that it was his turn. "You always do that to me, Cirroc. You always sit next to me and you always do that." But then he added, "I like coming in three hours later and seeing Rene and Armin almost made up."

"I like the overtime," Armin said, picking up on Colm's response. But then Armin always talks about how much overtime he makes; clearly it's on his mind a lot.

"Now what is there left for me to say?" Nana complained. "Is this going to happen every time I'm last?"

The cast then turned to a fan named Steve from North Hollywood. Steve wanted to know: where does the gravity on the space station come from? "It seems that the cups and things aren't floating up there in space.

Why is that?"

"The gravity comes from Paramount," Armin insisted.

The host then directed a question to Nana Visitor. Pointing out that she had worked with Angela Lansbury and appeared on such shows as EMPTY NEST, and L.A. LAW; he asked how DEEP SPACE NINE challenges her as an actor.

"The best part is doing the kind of work you want to do and working with all these actors. Everyone is really talented. The challenging part is the long hours."

### The Man Behind Quark

The moderator turned to Rene and Armin, asking about their characters and their relationship with one another. Rene said to Armin, "You always get the last word so I'll take this first. Actually you should all look forward to an episode upcoming where we're going to be married."

"He proposed, I accepted," Armin quipped. "He makes more than I do," Shimmerman added, once again bringing money into the conversation. Just like a Ferengi.

### Perspectives on Acting

An audience member asked Avery Brooks how he is trying to make his character different from the main characters in the other two STAR TREK series: Captain Kirk and Captain Picard.

Avery replied, "The worst thing an actor can do is try to repeat what someone else has already done. I am really trying to find myself in the role, making a transition from one character to another," he said, referring to his movement from the role of Hawk to his current role as Ben Sisko. "It's like being a musician: you can play anything. I can do anything."

The host turned to Terry Farrell, remarking, "You're from Iowa. This role must be vastly different from anything in Iowa."

Armin Shimmerman at Universal Studios Hollywood, November, 1993.    **Photo c 1994 Alvert L. Ortega**

Terry responded, "It's vastly different from anyplace in the United States; probably the world!"

Another fan asked Rene whether he prefers the role he had in BENSON to the role of Odo on DEEP SPACE NINE.

"When you're playing a role," Rene answered, "it seems to be that it's always the part you're playing that you love the best. That would be my immediate answer about Odo. I loved doing BENSON; I had a great time and I loved the character Clayton, but let's face it, he was a nitwit! Even though Odo is something of a curmudgeon, which is closer to who I actually am—you can ask all these people—I find him a much more interesting and sort of honorable character. I admire his tension and I love the character. I hope that I'm going to be doing it for a long time with all these wonderful actors."

## DS9 and the Next Generation

Colm Meaney was asked

whether he preferred working on NEXT GENERATION to DEEP SPACE NINE.

"That's a very difficult question," he began. "On the NEXT GENERATION I was around quite a bit and I was described as an irregular regular, sort of like a step-cousin. I had a lot of fun with those guys. But I enjoy being here, being in on the beginning of a show and seeing the show grow and gel—or un-gel as the case may be. We're very fortunate that we have a very good cast in terms of acting ability and also personality."

Siddig was asked about his career in London where he did a lot of directing in the theatre. He was asked whether he wants to continue directing now that he's working in the United States.

"Yes, but not on this show immediately. It's a bit hubristic to ask Rick Berman now—but I'd like to direct, maybe in year two." The host pointed out that if Jason Priestly can direct then Siddig should certainly be allowed to do so as well.

## Quark Again

A fan asked Armin Shimmerman how long he has to sit in the makeup chair and whether he ever gets antsy while the make-up is being applied.

Nana Visitor piped up, "Boy, does he get antsy! You do it in two stages, don't you?" she asked.

"Anger and extreme anger," Armin quipped. "It takes three hours. A lot of overtime! I've gotten used to it but hopefully the process will get shorter. I talked to Michael Dorn the other day. His used to take three hours and now it takes thirty-seven minutes. I'm hoping to beat his record some time."

"But Michael looks like that now," Rene remarked. "And that's what's going to happen to him," referring to Armin. "As you do the show you begin to look more and more like the character."

"Does anybody have a pail for him?" Armin asked.

A young boy asked Armin, "Do you think there's a little bit of your personality mixed up with

Quark's personality?

"None whatsoever," Armin insisted, but then he added seriously, "All actors bring a part of themselves to their roles and whatever part of me that is Quark has somehow risen to the top, yes."

## The Youngest Star Trek Cast Member

The moderator asked Cirroc, "You play an Army brat on the show, and that means you get to do a lot of rotten things. What kind of mischievous stuff do you do with your friend Nog?"

"He's played some tricks on me. We throw things on people while they're walking down the promenade. We really don't do that many tricks. He leads me into doing everything— my dad thinks that it's me doing everything but it's not me." Someone asked about the pail joke.

"Well, Odo lives in this pail," Cirroc began, "Nog and I went to retrieve it. He picked it up and threw it at me. I thought that Odo was inside it, and that

turned out to be a pretty funny scene." What Jake thought was Odo was actually oatmeal. That incident took place in the episode "Progress" in the first season.

One of the audience members asked about the projects in which the actors are involved when DEEP SPACE NINE is not filming.

"We spend so much time working on the series," Avery explained, "that a lot of us don't have much time to do other work. Although, certainly, everybody here is very active during the hiatus. I am the Artistic Director of the National Black Arts Festival, which happens in the summer. So there is a world beyond STAR TREK."

## The Face and the Voice

Rene Auberjonois was asked about a movie he has coming out on the USA channel.

"Maybe I do. I don't know. I've been in this business so long now that it's embarrassing the things that do show up. I'm in a movie—just out—called THE BALLAD OF LITTLE JOE. I also do a lot of cartoon voices; I do a lot of work for Disney and Hanna-Barbara. I also try to do something in the theatre whenever I'm free. Theatre is my first love and I try to do that when I have the opportunity."

The moderator pointed out that Rene was the voice of Chef Louie in THE LITTLE MERMAID. The cast wanted him to sing for them. Instead Avery just did a few lines in the voice of Chef Louie. "I sing for them in the dressing room, but not today," he said.

A young woman asked Terry Farrell whether she likes to watch the show on TV, because not all actors like to watch their performances on film.

"I only watch it when it's about my character," Terry said jokingly, "which means that I'll be busy next week."

## The Future of Deep Space Nine

Another audience member wanted to know if the

Rene Auberjonois at Universal Studios Hollywood, November, 1993.          Photo c 1994 Alvert L. Ortega

Colm Meany at Universal Studios Hollywood, November, 1993.

**Photo c 1994 Alvert L. Ortega**

1994 season of DEEP SPACE NINE would follow the same format as the first season or if they would be visiting more planets through the wormhole.

"People ask us questions about what is going to happen," said Rene, "and I think that all of us would say that every week we get the script and go, 'Whoa, that's interesting!' We don't know what's going to happen ahead of time . That makes it more of an adventure for us, I think. We're not very good at telling people what's going to happen because often we don't know ourselves."

"Also we're told that if we do we'll get in trouble," Avery added.

Colm Meaney was asked by the host how being an actor trained in Ireland has impacted his work in the United States.

"I'm not sure. The training I had in Ireland was good: I was at the Irish National Theatre part-time and I attended classes there. I also spent time doing small parts, so I was in a professional environment, getting a feel for a professional theatre. I was quite happy with the training."

Asked whether DIE HARD II was his first commercial success in the United States, Colm replied, "I wouldn't exactly call it my commercial success," since Colm was a supporting player in the film which had a rather large cast.

Avery Brooks was asked whether he liked baseball as much as Ben Sisko does.

"It's growing on me," he said. "That's pretty funny because when I first was told by the agency people about STAR TREK they asked: are you a baseball fan? I said I would let them know. When I got the job I said, 'I am now.' "My father played semi-professional baseball in the Negro Leagues so I've been around it all my life."

## Kira and Quark

Nana Visitor was asked what she does to prepare for the spirituality of her character.

"You know it's interesting," she said, "when I first

had the nose prosthetic put on I walked around Paramount. No one knew the show or what we were doing. They looked at me thinking, 'What is wrong with her nose?' It was a very interesting feeling because all of a sudden I felt like, 'Why are you looking at me like something's wrong?! That's the way my nose looks!' The spirituality is kind of the same thing. It's the earring. I put the earring on it's supposed to remind us of our Pagh, our spirituality. It actually pinches going on. I don't know what that means about the spirituality, but it certainly does remind me about that part of my character. The physicality of the earring on my ear gets that going for me."

Nana then was asked what she thinks about her character having a love affair with a Bajoran monk.

"It's not really a love affair," Nana said. "We kind of saw an orb thing in the future that maybe it will happen, so I don't really know what's going on. I know that there's an attraction, but I haven't seen him for awhile. Maybe Kira will never have a relationship that works out—she's just one of those women. I think I'm the only one that hasn't had a romantic interest on the show."

"Besides me," Armin piped in.

"Well, throwing Quark up against the wall, what could be more fun than that?" Kira insisted.

"I find that very romantic," Armin added as Quark came to the top again.

## A Variety of Interests

Another young lady in the audience wondered what the height requirement was for a Ferengi.

"Nobody's taller than I am," Armin stated, matter-of-factly.

Siddig was asked whether it was true that even though he's been in the United States for a year he is also a celebrity in England. He replied, "No. I've done some stuff, but I'm not a celebrity." Asked about the differences between being known in England and in the States he said, "I don't know

because I wasn't very well known in England. People recognized me but thought I was at dinner with them a few weeks ago or something—they thought they'd met me socially. There isn't much difference, I don't think [in the way celebrities are treated]. In England people run around and scream as much as they do here."

A fan asked Avery Brooks whether he would consider appearing at a STAR TREK convention now that he has finally gotten out and met the fans.

"The truth of the matter is that I really haven't had time. I'm sure that at some point I will, but I can't tell you when." Asked whether it was true that he's a jazz musician, Avery said, "I'm a musician up to a point. I grew up playing on the woodwinds, except for the flute and the piano. And I sing."

Asked whether he always knew he wanted to be in show business, Avery answered, "No, as a matter of fact. Art is simply a tool for talking about the world and I didn't start out in this piece of geography. I almost had to be brought here kicking and screaming, because we all do so many different things and, again, it's merely a way of discussing the world. Because I'm concerned about talking about the world, I'm concerned about what's happening in succeeding generations, I suppose that I made a choice, long ago, to be involved."

## Jake, Quark and Odo Answer...

Cirroc was asked whether it was difficult having to go to school while doing the series.

"It's kind of difficult. We go for twenty minutes while we're shooting, then we have a break and I go back for twenty minutes, until I get my three hours in. I'm in tenth grade right now."

"Quark is an offensive, sexist, and greedy alien, but I understand that you're a shy person," the host asked Armin. "Is this a part of you, deep down?"

Armin replied, "I do tend to think of myself as

Siddig el Fadil at Universal Studios Hollywood, November, 1993.

Terry Farrell at Universal Studios Hollywood, November, 1993.

**Photo c 1994 Alvert L. Ortega**

relatively shy. I imagine this is some sort of fantasy I've always wanted to act out somehow." Then he paused, and continued, "Oh, that was deep."

Asked whether there were any topical issues that any of the cast members would like to see the series touch on, Rene replied, "The series actually does touch on a lot of topical issues, none of which leap to mind right now while I'm talking to you. But we have had episodes which have reflected what is happening in Bosnia and there have been episodes which deal with, obliquely, things like the AIDS epidemic. I think that a number of our episodes really echo what's happening now.

"I think that what's interesting about STAR TREK is that it is not as much about the future as it is about how humanity deals [with the future]."

## The Origin of Major Kira

Nana Visitor was asked whether she was hired to replace Ensign Ro, the character played on NEXT GENERATION by Michelle Forbes.

"They thought, when they were writing the show, that they wanted Michelle Forbes to be the first officer. When she turned that down, they decided to rewrite the character, not as Ensign Ro but as Major Kira. The only similarity is that we're Bajoran women and we are aggressive. The characters are two different people; I was never trying to recreate my character from another actress's performance."

She also explained the pronunciation of her name. She said, "My mother is French and she says Nana [with a short sound on both a's]. Avery says Nana [with a long sound on the first a], and always has—it's my favorite pronunciation of my name. I'll accept anything."

## The Shape of Things

Rene was asked, as Security Officer Odo: since he can change his shape, into what would he like to shift, or would he like to shift someone else?

He replied, "Someone else I'd like to shift into? You mean like Robert Redford? If I could turn somebody else into something I would turn Quark into a footstool."

"Really?" Armin asked, to which Rene replied, "We'll talk about it later."

Rene then added, "People say, if Odo is so great at turning himself into a rat or a knapsack or a glass or whatever, why doesn't he make himself look a little better? Why doesn't he turn himself into Robert Redford? Then I wouldn't have gotten the part. Robert Redford would have gotten the part, so there you go."

## Down to Earth Interests

The cast members were asked to elaborate on their hobbies.

"My hobby, really, right now," Nana stated, "is my one-and-a-half year old son. If I'm not at work, I'm with Buster and my husband."

Armin stated, "I've spent most of my life trying to find out the secrets of Shakespeare. That's primarily my study. That's a hobby, I guess."

Colm Meaney seemed hesitant and then said, "I hang out, okay? I hang out. What's wrong with that? I also watch sports and play with this little girl down here, Brenda, my love," he added, referring to his young daughter. "When she gets real busy—like tomorrow, she's leaving me alone all day to go out to play with other friends—I just hang out. That's basically what I do."

Cirroc said, "I collect cards—baseball, basketball, stamps, and I play video games. Mortal Kombat and all of those. And I play basketball." He likes the Bulls but is disappointed that Michael Jordan left the team.

"I don't follow football or basketball or any of that stuff—it's too complicated to get into for me," Siddig explained. "I'll tell you about cricket if you really want to know about a boring, complicated game. I spend most of my time in local bars with Colm, here, drinking weak beer and talking about why we haven't got a decent hobby."

"It's hard to follow that," Rene began. "I ride my mountain bike, up in the hills. Actually I was up there this morning and I could see Universal Studios. And I'm a photographer."

"I don't have any hobbies. I don't have time!" Avery exclaimed. "I'm always doing something so I really haven't a hobby to speak of."

## Working on Deep Space Nine

The cast was asked what a normal work day on DEEP SPACE NINE is like, from morning until the end of shooting.

"It's different all the time," Terry explained. "Normal for me isn't very normal. I get two hours for hair and makeup; I don't get into uniform until after we've rehearsed. Then it really depends on how long Marcus has to light before we come in and start shooting the scene. That goes on all day and ends somewhere after twelve hours and before sixteen hours. But you just never know.

"Nana and I had a scene that I liked so much and they called me last night to tell me it was omitted. I'm very disappointed about that. So, it changes all the time.

"Sometimes you work four days a week and sometimes you work every day. Avery is there almost every day.

"The longest day I've had is twenty hours," Nana revealed. "That's a long work day."

## An Anecdote about Quark

Armin was asked whether he's ever been recognized in public without his makeup.

"Armin tells people," Terry Farrell stated, jumping in before Armin could say anything. "'No. Don't tell anybody what I look like, okay?' It rarely happens. I have been out with STAR TREK people before and it's wonderful to be overlooked. It truly is. I'll

Cirroc Lofton at Universal Studios Hollywood, November, 1993. **Photo c 1994 Alvert L. Ortega**

bore you all with a quick little anecdote. At the end of last season, four of us went out to dinner at a nice place, and a young man about six or seven came over to the table. The boy saw Rene and asked him if he was Odo, and Rene said 'yes.' Rene introduced the rest of the people at the table, including Nana Visitor and Terry Farrell.

"Then he said, 'and this is Armin Shimerman. He plays Quark.' 'No way!' the boy replied. But I rather like not being recognized."

So Armin did get the last word, just as Rene predicted. The show came to a close as the host thanked the cast of DEEP SPACE NINE for sharing their Saturday with Universal Studios.

# CHARACTER PROFILE:

# COMMANDER BEN SISKO

*— Alex Burleson*

Since his arrival on the space station Deep Space Nine, Commander Benjamin Sisko has become more rested and relaxed than he had been in recent years. Sisko had fully dealt with the death of his wife, Jennifer, who was killed three years earlier aboard the USS Saratoga when the vessel was attacked by the Borg. The attack occurred in the vicinity of the M5 Red Dwarf star known as Wolf 359. The Borg ship encountered an armada of 40 Federation starships, including Klingon ships, and destroyed them all, resulting in a death toll near ten thousand. Ben Sisko, then First Officer of the Saratoga, along with his son, Jake, were among the few survivors. The massacre, known as the Battle of Wolf 359, occurred on Stardate 43997.

Captain Jean-Luc Picard of the USS Enterprise had been kidnapped and surgically altered to become Locutus of Borg. Picard was held for six days until he was rescued by his own First Officer, Will Riker. With the help of Second Officer Data, they were able to stop the Borg ship from destroying Terra, although the semi-conscious Picard provided the vital clue they needed to defeat the Borg.

The Wolf 359 system is the third closest star, followed by the two binary components of the Alpha Centauri system, six light years from Proxima. Rigel Kentaurus is Alpha Centauri A, locked into an orbit around a common gravity well with Alpha B, both G5 Yellow Dwarfs, comparable to Sol. This system is followed by Barnard's Star, the first

Avery Brooks in uniform at 1992 Deep Space Nine Press Conference

**Photo c 1994 Alvert L. Ortega**

measured by stellar parallax, leading to the creation of the term parsec, or parallax second. A parsec is one arcsecond or second of arc on a star chart. After Bernard's M5 Red Dwarf, comes Wolf 359, with Tau Ceti rounding out Terra's surrounding defense parameter—this demonstates how close the Borg got to Earth, astronomically speaking.

The USS Melbourne, under the command of Admiral J.P. Hanson, was destroyed with the loss of all hands. Lt. Commander Sisko and his then 9-year-old son, Jake, made it into the Saratoga's escape pod in the nick of time, but Jennifer was killed by a crashing tritanium bulkhead. Sisko refused to address his feelings in the aftermath of the incident. Ben used his late Vulcan captain as an example and buried the many white-hot emotions beneath the surface. Memories of the Saratoga haunt him every waking and sleeping moment; the Bolian pulled his body to safety but left his mind and his soul in that room, reeling from the screams of the dying as he watched the only thing that made his life worth living vanish. The black hole that opened in his heart sucked away his will until nothing mattered, nothing except for that one gift that Jennifer had left him—the child who looked more and more like his mother each day. Ben had many demons to wrestle with before he and Jake could have a normal life.

Starfleet became concerned that Ben had let his career stall watching starships being assembled at the Martian Utopia Planetia Shipyards. The shipyards are located on a plain on Mars, about 2,000 kilometers east of Olympus Mons. Starfleet ordered Sisko to take command of the former Cardassian ore processing space station in orbit around the planet Bajor. That world was recently abandoned by the ruthless Cardassian overlords who raped and plundered Bajor and left the Bajoran people to try to rebuild their civilization.

## Tear of the Prohpet

Sisko accepted the assignment to Deep Space Nine under protest and was ready to bolt when he saw the condition of the station. He applied for a job as a professor at a Terran university and was seriously considering leaving Starfleet so he could raise Jake on Earth. Ben and Jake arrived at Deep Space Nine on Stardate 46379.1.

Ben's life would be changed forever by his visit to meet the Bajoran spiritual leader, Kai Opaka. She entrusted him with an "orb," known as the "Tear of the Prophet." The orb enabled him to relive the first time he met his late wife, only to him it was not just a vision—it was real. The orb also led Sisko and Dax to find the link with the Denorios Belt which led to the discovery of the stable vertiron wormhole connecting the Alpha Quadrant with the Gamma Quadrant, some 70,000 light years away—420 trillion miles from the farthest outpost in the Federation.

Sisko encountered the

beings who constructed the orbs and built the wormhole. These beings, whom the Bajorans worship as "Prophets of the Celestial Temple," took the form of people in Ben's memory. As he understands what we are to the beings, he realizes what he has been missing. He is forced to relive the horror of the firestorm on the Saratoga and is finally able to accept the fact that emotionally he has never left the side of Jennifer's body. He saw her silent face in his dreams and in his waking hours. In the time it takes to blink an eye he is back aboard the burning starship, his hand on hot metal, ready to give his life in an instant if only it would restore life to the person who meant more to him than life itself.

Only his love for his son (and the strength of the Bolian who dragged Ben from Jennifer's body) allowed Sisko to get to the escape pod. When Jake awoke in his hospital room and was informed by Ben of his mother's death, the boy noticed a sad, almost sedate manner in his

father. This would continue until Ben was reborn by his visit to the wormhole. Ben had let a part of him die and the chance to see Jennifer again allowed "her" to help him grieve and finally reach acceptance. He was able to forgive Picard, be a better father to Jake, and to learn to love life again.

## The Long Journey

Sisko was given a new lease on life. He developed his detached—almost maddening—calm command style after an incident that occurred in his first year at Starfleet Academy. An unannounced drill caught him by surprise and he panicked. He then learned that the best way to deal with a crisis situation was to keep his head and remain calm. This leads many unsuspecting adversaries to underrate him, as his calm demeanor belies what is going on in his mind from moment to moment. Enterprise Captain Picard is widely known for his similar cool under fire, but

Sisko is even more drawn to the result his calm has on those around him, especially the junior officers under his command.

The Saratoga's late captain, a Vulcan named Storil, had a profound influence on Sisko's life. Ben marveled at the way the Vulcan could give his last orders with the same voice he would have used to ask for a routine fuel report. Benjamin affected a similar calm as he was forced to take command of the ship and organize the evacuation of the civilians and surviving crew. He then went on his journey to find Jennifer and Jake in their quarters, a journey which would not end at the rescue of his son and the death of his wife; the trip ends with Sisko's fulfillment of the Bajoran prophecy that a non-believer would find the temple and save the prophets from Cardassian attack.

Sisko shook off the accolades that accompanied his position of "Emissary" in the Bajoran religion, and was extremely annoyed by the constant need to let Bajoran Kai and Vedeks read his "pagh," or life-force, each time they encounter him. Sisko has noted the parallel between his attempt to rebuild his life and Bajor's efforts to repair the damage done to them by the Cardassians. He learns to interact with his new crew; his relationship with each of them reflects the his transformation in the wormhole.

## A Man of Many Talents

Sisko is an amateur astronomer and has taken to studying Bajoran constellations. His favorite is named "The Runners." He said that he always wondered whether they were running toward or away from something. He is a skilled chef, a trait he learned from his father. He was especially fond of his father's aubergine stew, a dish that he often makes for Jake and Dax. Sisko is a poet at heart. He has a love of baseball and has spent hours on holodecks recreating games. He speaks with great reverence for a game that ceased to exist

Avery Brooks

**Photo c 1994 Alvert L. Ortega**

centuries before he was born. Sisko has developed a relationship with some of the players, which proved to their advantage when an alien being took the form of Harmon "Buck" Bukai, the shortstop, third baseman for the London Kings who broke Joe Dimaggio's 56 game hitting streak in 2026.

Sisko is more than willing to stand up for his people and has publicly defended Odo and Dax when each was charged with murder. Sisko and Kira have often butted heads over matters in which Bajoran and Starfleet interests differ, but the two have managed to produce a working relationship based on mutual respect that allows them to function as a team. Their antagonism was brought out when an alien probe produced a psychological effect on the crew, as telepathic psy-art produced delusions among those affected. Odo was immune and was forced to find a solution as the factions split up with Kira, Dax and Julian teaming up against Sisko and Miles O'Brien, each group out to kill the other. Odo was forced to make Bashir find a cure, while dealing with Kira's bizarre personality traits and everyone else's odd behavior. Afterwards, Sisko felt some shame at the way he had acted and quickly moved to restore good feelings by asking Kira to assist him with a report on the incident that began with hail from a Klingon ship which was infected with the "art" in the Gamma Quadrant.

## Taking a Stand

Sisko is quietly gaining the respect of Bajoran and Federation alike with his calm, measured response to a crisis and his attempts to balance Bajoran mysticism and religion with the need to teach science and other disciplines. Sisko stood up to Vedek Winn, informing the Bajoran that he was neither the devil and nor their enemy. Kira was forced to admit Sisko was not a devil, an event that brought a rare smile to Sisko's face.

Sisko is learning to deal with Jake' transitiion into adolescence. Sisko is concerned about Jake's friendship with Nog; he is insulted that Nog's father, Rom, is equally concerned about Jake's influence on Nog. Jake has a girlfriend—a Dabo girl who works for Quark. Ben has had a harder time dealing with this fact than he has with accepting the fact that Jake is not interested in joining Starfleet when he comes of age. Ben is at his best in paternal mode, forcing Jake to study Klingon opera, as Ben had to when he was young. Jake asked his father why he should have to study something that seemed so useless. Ben fumbled for an answer, suggesting Jake might be together with Klingons on a job somewhere.

A telling example of Sisko's interpersonal abilities involves the case of a terraformer who lost his life in the creation of a new star. Ben had found himself in an uncomfortable position. He admired the egotistical planetmaker and was unnerved to discover that the beautiful young woman he had fallen in love with was in fact married to the older scientist. The wife of the great terraformer was actually an empathic projection telepath, meaning that she would fall into a coma while her subconscious projected an image of herself. This unconscious image is the one who fell in love with Ben. Even though the woman is cold to Ben and remembers nothing, her telepathic image remembers everything and is banished when the woman awakens.

## Klingon Poetry

The proud, defiant scientist then gave his own life to spare her the continued pain of a life-long mating to an egotist, the very pain that drove her into the coma. As he died, the wild scientist sparked an emotion in Sisko by mentioning an old Klingon poem. Sisko understood the reference. The terraformer died in response to the "Tale of Kang." The poem went into vivid detail on how great it was to die at the peak of one's existence—to

pass this veil beloved, yet never to have been seen in tragic decline. The tragic Shakespearean lilt of Kang led him to perceive that there would be nothing worse than being an ancient warrior, pitied because he had slain all of his enemies, leaving him no more worlds to conquer. The scientist refused to allow himself to be pitied, thus finishing a magnificent stellar first-time-ever event—the artificial creation of a star—to end his career on a perfect high note.

Ben recognized the poem when it was first quoted, and when the duty officer did not understand suicidal planetmaker's ramblings, Sisko quietly stated "Klingon poetry," and promised to deliver the scientist's obituary to the Daystrom Institute. An egotist to the end, the planetmaker had written it himself.

Sisko has varied views of his crew and his duties, and at any time they are subject to revision based on the circumstances and the facts. This Starfleet style chaffs Odo and Kira, but each are learning to find ways to get around the red tape and get the support they need. Only in extraordinary situations do they find outright conflict among the bridge crew.

The one unifying factor so far has been the appearance of the "Q" entity, who arrived with Vash, a Terran archeologist (and former lover of Jean-Luc Picard) who was brought back from the Gamma Quadrant by a runabout. Vash had preceded Ben and Jadzia to the Gamma Quadrant accepting an offer made by Q three years ago in Picard's Ready Room on the Enterprise. The entire crew of Deep Space Nine became united in their hatred of Q.

## Sisko and Dax

Benjamin Sisko first met Curzon Dax, who served as his mentor, years before. At that time, Dax was a male. While Ben knew that Dax would join him on DS9, he was surprised—and somewhat amused—to learn that Dax

was now a beautiful young woman rather than the elderly man who previously had guided Ben. Whenever Sisko sees Julian or another young man make an attempt at seduction, he is reminded of a kindly old man, smiling with the same bemused expression as Jadzia. Curzon Dax was a hard-drinking, two-fisted fighter, a womanizer and borderline sexist. Can one still be sexist when one has been both sexes and shares memories of being at times a boy, a girl, a mother and a father? Dax has been all things at different times. Sisko is still learning to adapt to the new being named Jadzia Dax.

Ben first met Jadzia when she and Julian reported for duty aboard Deep Space Nine. It was not long before Sisko was defending his old friend when Dax was accused of treason, conspiracy and murder, acts which occurred when she was still Curzon Dax. Dax was actually guilty only of adultery with the late General Tundro's widow, who finally confessed in

Avery Brooks and Terry Farrell.

Photo c 1994 Alvert L. Ortega

order to give Dax the alibi.. The widow's confession soiled her reputation but kept alive the legend of the general who was killed in an ambush after he had betrayed his own troops.

## Keeping Her Silence

Jadzia Dax was prepared to give her combined lives to protect the general's name, his widow's reputation, and the honor and respect of all Trills, who willingly agree to assume responsibility for crimes that were committed by previous hosts. When an armed attack by a renegade Trill occurred, Benjamin shot Dax with a phaser without shooting Jadzia. The Dax symbiont had been surgically removed and placed into the renegade Trill's body. The Trill felt that he had been denied Dax. Sisko used his friendship with Dax to confuse the Trill body thief. Dax will always carry part of him inside her, along with the memories of Toban Dax, Curzon Dax and all the other seven host/symbiont combinations.

Sisko often seeks out Dax's serene wisdom and sense of humor. She noted that Curzon appeared to appreciate Ben's baseball stories more than he actually did, but she really does enjoy Benjamin's company and is gratified wtih the time they have spent together in the two lifetimes. Dax is saddened to know that, barring unseen accident, she will outlive Sisko and all her other compatriots on Deep Space Nine. Jadzia will eventually die but Dax will live on. Dax has buried numerous hosts, foes, children, families, friends and co-workers. Like Spock, Data and perhaps Odo, she must deal with short paraThis is a special sadness reserved for the Trill.

Ben is amused by Dr. Bashir's outrageous attempts to romance the combined life form. Sisko and Dax were the first known visitors to the Gamma Quadrant. It was later discovered that an archeologist named Vash preceded them with help from the "Q" entity. Dax and Ben disliked Q because

he used his great power for his own amusement while other life forms suffered. They have seen enough tin-horn dictators and beings who feel they have the right to tell everyone else how to live. Ben and Dax's history together affects how the others perceive them, and shades their perceptions as both sides seek compromise.

## Sisko and Kira

The relationship between Sisko and Kira is one of the most complex on the space station. The feisty Bajoran freedom fighter spent her life trying to free her people from a powerful empire, only to see her planet invite in another, if somewhat more benevolent, empire in the form of the Federation. When Sisko arrives, he evicts her from the prefect's office, which she had taken as her own after Gul Dukat fled the ore processing station. She notices the hate in Sisko's eyes as he heads off to encounter Picard, whom he is unable to separate from his memories of

Locutus of Borg, the leader of the Borg massacre at Wolf 359.

She is later surprised when Sisko pitches in to help her clean up and begins to re-evaluate him after he is summoned by the Kai and chosen as the "Emissary" to the prophets in the "Celestial Temple," a stable vertiron wormhole. The events were similar to a dream shared by Kira and Sisko, about Kai Opaka and the orbs. Opaka was a central figure in Kira's life and Sisko's relationship with the Kai helped improve relations between Kira and Sisko.

Kira had made a few remarks about Starfleet commanders in general when Sisko had first arrived, but he immediately gained her respect by standing up to her and blackmailing Quark. He was called off to Bajor to meet with the Kai where he received "The Tear of the Prophets." Sisko and Dax each have a vision which helps them understand of the beings in the wormhole. Kira later encountered an orb during her stay with Vedek Bareil at the monastery on Bajor. The beings that the Kai, Kira and other Bajorans worship as the prophets of the Celestial temple are just aliens to Sisko. He teaches them about linear time but the Kai does not want him to share his knowledge , stating that it is best if one does not "look into the eyes of one's own gods."

## Religious Manipulation

This complex intermix of religion and science has led to heated exchanges between Kira and Sisko. For example, Major Kira initially backed Vedek Winn's attempt to intimidate Keiko into changing her school curriculum. After Winn's bombing of the school and the attempted assassination of Bareil , Ben was then able to get the Bajoran nationals to stand behind the Deep Space Nine crew.

This support proved vital when "The Circle" began their conspiracy which, for awhile, cost Kira her job as First Officer and Deep Space Nine Liaison to Bajor. Eventually, however, it helped forge the friendships between Kira and her crewmates as one by one, each came to her quarters to let her know how much she means to them. This was best illustrated by Sisko, as he stood up to Minister Jaro and complained about her removal. He vowed to Kira that he would get her back and even went as far as to mount an armed rescue attempt to save her from the fundamentalists. She was being tortured by fellow Bajorans when Sisko, Bashir and the rescue party acted on "deputy" Quark's tip and arrived just in time to save her.

Major Kira joined Dax in exposing the conspiracy, just as it became clear that the anti-Cardassian "Circle" would actually be handing Bajor back to the Cardassians, who were secretly providing weapons to help the "Circle" drive out the Federation. The Cardassians wanted to return and gain control of the stable wormhole which has made Bajor much more valuable than it was in the past.

Kira and Sisko share a dislike for the Cardassians, yet each has done his or her duty when faced with the fact that they had to deal in a civil fashion with Cardassians. This is a character trait both Sisko and Kira share with Miles O'Brien.

## Dr. Julian Bashir

Sisko takes a perverse pleasure in forcing Julian to endure what he, himself, had to endure in his youth. He made the doctor escort some alien ambassadors around and Commander Sisko pointed out how Curzon Dax used to do the same to him. The task proved up to Julian's talents when the young doctor's quick thinking was able to save the life of the Vulcan, Bolian and female alien ambassador during a flash fire.

Ben was upset with Julian when he spoke offhandedly about the commander's decision to help a race of prisoners escape from their planetary jail. Sisko, Kira and Julian had survived the crash of the runabout Yangtze Kiang but Kai Opaka was killed. The Kai was revived and forced to remain behind on that prison planet, a planet tortured by unending war fought by immortal combatants, men and women who have been forged into pure vessels of hate. Kai Opaka feels obligated to try to help these people. The parallels with Bajor are striking. The Kai remains alive, in forced exile, until Julian can find a way to return her to Bajor without killing her. Sisko is learning to respect the young doctor and takes his arrogance with a grain of salt.

## Odo and Quark

Sisko has told Odo he likes him because he is blunt. He always knows where Odo stands on an issue. He also appreciates Odo's obvious zeal for justice and, especially in relation to security. Yet Ben has to deal with the fact that Odo is often more concerned with pure justice than with the enforce-ment of rules and regulations. Odo was not optimistic about having a Starfleet officer in command; he was prepared to dislike Sisko immediately. That bias was encouraged when Sisko violated the constable's 'No weapons on the Promenade' rule. Odo was, however, impressed with the way in which Sisko blackmailed Quark and manipulated the Ferengi. Odo gained respect for Sisko when the commander gave him the authority over Starfleet security operations.

Sisko used Ferengi psychology in his first encounter with the owner of the gambling casino, and surprisingly, he gained Quark's respect. Sisko understood the need for a plea bargain in order to force Quark's hand. Quark had expected his words to win his nephew Nog's freedom, yet when Sisko blackmailed him, Quark respected him. Sisko does not trust Quark; he knows enough about Ferengi intelligence to understand how to interact, but never to forget, he is dealing with a Ferengi.

## Miles & Keiko

Sisko liked Miles O'Brien at first sight and has found the former Enterprise transporter chief to be a true miracle worker, able to coax Cardassian equipment into doing the impossible. Sisko and Miles have a close relationship and he is glad to have such a capable engineer, especially when the station goes on Red Alert and Miles finds his skills put to the test with the lives of every being on the station hanging in the balance.

Sisko was pleased when Keiko volunteered to open a school on Deep Space Nine. He had worried about Jake being forced to study alone with his computer and thought a school would help keep the children on the station out of trouble. Ben provided computers and space for the school, and his example of sending Jake helped encourage other parents to give the school a chance.

Keiko was happy that Sisko stood up for her when the fundamentalist Bajoran, Vedek Winn, attempted to shut down the school because teaching about the science of the wormhole offended Bajoran spiritual beliefs. Some parents objected to the study of vertiron particles, which were artificially generated by the beings who live in the wormhole. To some Bajorans this is blasphemy since the beings are worshipped as prophets on Bajor and the wormhole in the Denetrios Belt is regarded as the "Celestial Temple." Sisko was able to enlist the help of Vedek Bareil to fend off Winn's attempt to shut down Keiko's school. Sisko then saved Bareil from an assassin that Winn had sent in an attempt to ensure that she would be the next Kai.

## Jake Sisko

The relationship between Ben and Jake is very complex and has been tested by the demands of duty and the fact that both father and son are still dealing with the death of Jennifer Sisko. Sisko has strived to be Jake's friend as well as his father, yet Ben feels that he neglected his son when he was blinded by grief for his wife. Ben felt guilty about putting Jennifer and Jake at risk on the Saratoga, but his transformation in the wormhole helped restore the father Jake had lost when he lost his mother. Sisko became a whole person again, one capable of being the father Jake wanted and needed.

The two enjoy baseball in the holosuites and Ben is a very active parent, offering a solid role model as he forces Jake to do his homework and improve himself. Ben is not afraid to show his feelings, kissing an embarrassed Jake on the forehead or hugging him on the Promenade. Jake is glad to have his dad back. The two are rediscovering a feeling of family.

## The Shadow of Jean-Luc Picard

When Sisko arrived at Bajor to take command of Deep Space Nine, he encountered Jean-Luc Picard for the first time. . .

that is, as Picard. Sisko had met him before—in battle. When Picard had been kidnapped and transformed by the Borg into Locutus of Borg, Sisko knew intellectually that Picard was not to blame for his forced actions, yet emotionally he could not separate Picard from the being that killed Jennifer. Picard had not met another survivor of Wolf 359. Sisko later realized he had added to Picard's pain and felt a deep sense of regret for reopening the painful wound. He behaved poorly, yet at the time, the events of Wolf 359 was still replaying constantly in his mind.

It was not until Ben encountered the beings in the wormhole that he was able to overcome his inability to accept Jennifer's death. This dramatic catharsis is evident in his second meeting with Picard. Sisko withdrew his request for a transfer as he finally realized how the Borg attack affected Picard as well; he realized that Picard's grief and his own were very similar. Ben finally understood that

Picard remembered all the deaths in detail and he felt responsible for each and every loss. Picard realized that Ben had lost his wife in the tragedy and vowed to do his best to help Ben and Jake whenever he could; helping them eased his own demons as well. The two parted as friends and Ben Sisko had at last put the events of Wolf 359 in past.

Avery Brooks and Cirroc Lofton.

Photo c 1994 Alvert L. Ortega

# ACTOR PROFILE

# AVERY BROOKS

The actor who plays Commander Sisko on DEEP SPACE NINE has an interesting background for the character. He was born and raised in Indiana and his father had been in the Negro baseball league in the 1940s. But like Avery, his father had a powerful singing voice. Brooks told TV GUIDE, "My father had a voice that shook the walls like thunder. He sang for a very famous gospel group named Wings Over Jordan. My mother was a pianist, organist, choral conductor and one of the first black women to get a master's degree in music from Northwestern. My uncle was one of the original Delta Rhythm Boys."

His higher education included taking classes and securing degrees at Oberlin College, Indiana University and then Rutgers University where he became the first black to achieve a Master of Fine Arts degree in acting and directing, which made the first TV role he gained notoriety from (Hawk in SPENSER FOR HIRE) that much more unusual.

Prior to appearing in SPENSER FOR HIRE, Brooks spent ten years on the stage in a traveling production of the powerful play "Paul Robeson" which was written by playwright Phillip Hayes Dean. Avery Brooks performed in the play all across the country, from the Westwood Playhouse in Los Angeles to the Kennedy Center in our nation's capital and even on Broadway. He reprised the role in another play, "Are You Now Or Have You Ever Been?" in 1978 when the play was staged both on and off Broadway.

## Malcolm X— The Musical

But Paul Robeson was by no means his only experience acting on the stage. Possessed of a powerful singing voice, he played Malcolm X in an operatic treatment of the black activist's life in "X: The Life And Times of Malcolm X." This was staged by the American Music Theatre festival and written by Anthony Davis. Also on the musical front, Brooks has worked with such notable jazz performers as Butch Morris, Henry Threadgill, Jon Hendricks, Joseph Jarman and Lester Bowie.

Brooks has avoided playing sterotypical roles and while rehearsing for the Malcolm X musical, he was sent on a TV audition by his agent and when he arrived the script didn't even have a name for the character, just a description as "The Black Dude in a Pink Hat." He was suggested for the part even after he had appeared on SPENSER FOR HIRE, perhaps because some producers were already trying to typecast him in the role of tough blacks. Brooks made certain he was never asked to audition for such a role again.

His theatrical credits include many other roles, including in plays by the Bard himself. Brooks had the lead in "Othello" when it was staged at the Folger Shakespeare Theatre in Washington, D.C. and for the New York Shakespeare Festival, Avery was featured in the plays "A Photograph" by Ntozake Shange as well as "Spell #7."

Drawing on his musical background, Avery Brooks hosted the documentary THE MUSICAL LEGACY OF ROLAND HAYES. He has also done a great deal of work for the Smithsonian's Black American culture program.

On Public Broad-casting's American Play-house series, Brooks starred in "Solomon Northup's Odyssey." He also received a Cable ACE Award for his performance as Uncle Tom on Showtime's production of UNCLE TOM'S CABIN.

But of course Brooks

first achieved public notoriety in 1985 as the hard-edged character Hawk, plating opposite Robert Urich, in SPENSER FOR HIRE. This eventually led to a short-lived spin-off series A MAN CALLED HAWK in 1989. Although both series were canceled, Brooks returned to play the character of Hawk in a made-for-cable Spencer for Hire TV movie in 1993.

## Casting the Lead

Although the premiere episode "Emissary" had largely been written before Avery Brooks was cast, exactly what type of actor would be right in the role had yet to be determined. A variety of performers read for the part including Siddig El Fadil who was cast instead as Dr. Bashir. Although at one point the producers considered having a female commander, this idea was altered to have Sisko's second in command, Major Kira, be a woman, although in the first episode she makes it clear that she believes that she should have been in charge instead of him.

The race of the actor was not a factor in the role and in fact thus far in the series Sisko's race has never even been referred to. Avery Brooks originally seemed an odd choice to some people as he was largely known to TV audiences as the street thug Hawk on SPENSER FOR HIRE, a character as far away from Avery's real personality as Sisko is from Hawk's. Unlike on SPENSER FOR HIRE, Brooks does not shave his head for his part on DEEP SPACE NINE.

In describing his character, the actor states, "He's not afraid to speak about how he feels. He's a deep thinker but, yeat, a quick one. He makes decisions very quickly. He also has a great sense of humor. He's curious about everything."

## A Family Man

Regarding what Avery Brooks is like to work with, Nana Visitor once mentioned that, because their trailers are next to each other, when they're called to the set she likes to quietly follow him so that she can listen to him singing to himself because he has such a great voice. She also mentioned the time that she was at the food table and said to Avery that she'd love it if they had spice cake and two hours later discovered that Avery had told this to one of the assistant directors who proceded to try to find spice cake for her. "Avery had everyone looking for spice cake! And he walks onto the sound stage and he knows everyone's name, first and last, and that's a big crew, a big company, and he knows the guest stars' names. He's such a gentleman. He's wonderful with his children, we see them when they come to the set. I have the utmost respect for him."

While working on DEEP SPACE NINE, Brooks remains associated with Rutgers University where he is a tenured 20 year professor of theater, and he still teaches occasionally at the Mason Gross School of the Arts where he is a professor of theater. "While teaching at Rutgers, I sang with such jazz artists as Jon Henricks, Butch Morris, and Lester Bowie. For years I straddled the fence between the academic and the performance," he explained.

Avery is the father of three children named Ayana, Asante and Cabral. His wife is an assistant dean at Rutgers and his principal residence remains in New Jersey in spite of the months he must spend in Hollywood working on the series. While this fact is known, whatever difficulties this may cause for him Brooks remains tight-lipped about and during the interview with him which appeared in the January 15, 1994 issue of TV GUIDE, when the subject of the long distance relationship with his family was raised, the actor made it clear that he did not consider it an appropriate subject for discussion.

Avery has become close friends with his young co-star, Cirroc Lofton, and in the 1993 Hollywood Christmas parade Cirroc rode in a car along with Avery and Brook's oldest son, Cabral. Brooks told TV GUIDE, "Cirroc is very much a part of my family. As a matter of fact, people are always asking me, 'Is he your son?' We're that close."

Regarding the criticism Brooks experienced when he starred in A MAN CALLED HAWK, due to the violent nature of the show, the actor is very articulate in expressing his point of view over an issue which has become even more publicized recently. He told TV GUIDE, "I find it incredibly irresponsible and ultimately ludicrous to suggest that television is somehow responsible for problems that we've faced for decades, for centuries. We live in a country whose very history is violent. In many ways it was founded with violent acts, yes? We miss the mark when we ask the film and television industries to do what we cannot do ourselves. Our problems were not brought on by THE RIFLEMAN. And if we cannot teach our children the difference between fiction and reality, then those problems lie with us."

# CHARACTER PROFILE

# JAKE SISKO

Raised primarily in the field as the son of a Starfleet officer, young Jake Sisko may have been born on Earth— but he has no memory of that planet whatsoever, beyond that derived from holodeck simulations. At a mere fourteen years of age, he's been around the galaxy, and then some, long before he arrived with his father, Commander Benjamin Sisko, at the space station designated by Starfleet as Deep Space Nine.

Jake has been with his father on four completely different starships (including the ill-fated Saratoga) and has lived on at least two alien planets before this, his father's latest assignment. He's sharp and alert, Jake is, but still more than a bit unsure of himself, not only because of his youth but because of the transient quality of his life to date. This has led him to devise and adopt his own surefire social survival skills when arriving in any new territory. He knows, by instinct at this point, how to find a place to fit in and who he can relate to. He's even managed to do this, remarkably enough, in the dark and winding corridors of Deep Space Nine.

# DEEP SPACE NINE CREW BOOK

Cirroc Lofton in uniform at 1992 Deep Space Nine press conference.

**Photo c 1994 Alvert L. Ortega**

## Opposites Attract

It may be hard to believe, especially for his straight laced father Benjamin, but Jake has become fast friends with a Ferengi— Nog, the teenaged son of the crafty Quark's dimwitted brother Rom. Sometimes their activities together are harmless, like watching females arrive at the docking bay or the Promenade. But as might be imagined, they've also managed to get into trouble a few times, like the instance in which they afflicted some diners on the Promenade with a harmless but annoying alien organism which causes its victims' skin to change into a wide variety of rainbow hues in a matter of a few seconds. (Needless to say, Odo was not amused.)

Sometimes their friendship leads to awkward moments: Jake's loyalty, one of his best qualities really, leads him at one point to support Nog's absurd schoolroom lie that his homework was stolen by Vulcans! For this and other reasons, his father has frowned on Jake's association with Nog, even going so far as to ban their friendship outright. But Benjamin Sisko relaxed this attitude somewhat after discovering that Jake was secretly helping Nog learn to read after his father Rom denied the Ferengi boy permission to attend Keiko O'Brien's new school on the station because the Nagus frowned on such relations between Ferengi and aliens.

Still, Jake is really a lonely boy. It doesn't help much that his mother was killed during the battle with the Borg that destroyed his father's ship, the Saratoga. This colors his perceptions of everything in his short life. Secretly, he doesn't care much for this spacefaring life, for he undoubtedly realizes that his mother would in all likelihood still be alive if their family had stayed on Earth.

## Father and Son Together

Almost obsessed with the planet of his origin, he thrives in holodeck recreations of Earth settings, like the riverside pier that he and his father were relaxing on when the Starfleet ship carrying them arrived at Deep Space Nine. These holodeck fantasies are his only link to the past that he dreams of, and the future he hopes for, on Earth. There's not much else for him to do, except go to school and study; the other children that his father promised would be living on the station are few and far between, with Nog turning out to be his only real friend so far. And even after the tutoring incident, Benjamin Sisko still sees the Ferengi boy as a bad influence— far from the way the faithful Jake perceives this important friendship.

Jake has made friends with someone else—a young Dabo Girl who works for Quark. Jake is tutoring her and when he confesses that he's interested in her, Commander Sisko is not exactly an understanding father. Ben is a bit more forgiving, though, when Jake confess-

Cirroc Lofton and Armin Shimmerman.

es that he's not interested in joining Starfleet when he gets older, although he hasn't yet decided just what it is he wants to do. Whatever it is, he doubts that it will have anything to do with Klingon opera in spite of his father's insistence that learning it as his teacher insists could prove beneficial to him some day.

Despite that natural father/son conflict, Benjamin and Jake Sisko are actually very close, sharing an interest in baseball and other Earth matters. Even though Benjamin Sisko can be strict and foreboding, Jake knows that he can turn to him at times of trouble; the core of their relationship is a very real honesty, and the bond forged by their shared loss of Jennifer Sisko, Jake's mother.

# ACTOR PROFILE

# CIRROC LOFTON

The young actor featured each week on DEEP SPACE NINE is a natural resident of Los Angeles. He became interested in acting when he was quite young and appeared in elementary school productions, including one where he played Martin Luther King, Jr. His first professional work was at age nine in an educational film titled "Agency for Instructional Technology." He was discovered by a professional photographer who saw the youth playing in a park with his family.

On television he could have been seen even before DEEP SPACE NINE in TV commercials. The commercials he appeared in were for such products as Kellogg's Rice Krispies, Tropicana Orange Juice as well as for McDonalds. In 1992 Cirroc made his big screen debut in the movie BEETHOVEN in a small role.

"I like being other people," Cirroc told STARLOG. "I'm really an actor all the time. Before being discovered in the part I was always a comedian and was also involved in drama. I feel everyday living is acting. So I've really enjoyed it so far because it's still me, but I'm being recognized now."

Cirroc Lofton.

**Photo c 1994 Alvert L. Ortega**

For each callback he got there were fewer and fewer boys until finally it was down to Cirroc and one other young actor. He says that the casting director winked at him after his final test as a silent approval and he knew he had the part.

Cirroc Lofton is a typical teenage boy whose interests include riding his bicycle and playing basketball. While working on the weekly TV series he goes to school on set with a tutor and is required to devote at least three hours a day to his studies. Cirroc feels that his own relationship with his father is very similar to that of Jake and Ben Sisko, who are very close and can talk to each other easily.

Between the end of the first season and the beginning of the second, Lofton grew a few inches until now he stands a lanky five foot ten, nearly as tall as Avery Brooks, but he still has the youthful appearance of most 15 year olds so the height change isn't as noticeable.

## The Big Audition

His initial tryout for the role of Jake Sisko was a mass audition in which two hundred other young male actors turned out.

## Learning his Craft

Because Avery Brooks is also a teacher of the theatrical arts he has taken Cirroc under his wing and coached him so that the youth has continued to learn about his craft through more than just experience.

In describing his work on the series and in discussing the various episodes, Cirroc states, "I really don't have any favorites. My acting is better in some than in others. As time progressed I felt more comfortable. I learned more and felt more comfortable as it went on. So I guess the newer episodes are more my favorites because I've improved as an actor."

Jake's counterpart on the show is his friend, Nog, the Ferengi boy, who is played by Aron Eisenberg, an actor in his mid-twenties. But Cirroc says that in the Ferengi makeup Aron looks like he's the same age as Jake is.

Regarding his future, Cirroc wants to continue acting but go to college as well. Although for a time he was thinking about being a doctor, now he's decided that he wants to make a career out of acting while still getting a college degree.

Cirroc Lofton

Photo c 1994 Alvert L. Ortega

Nana Visitor in uniform as Major Kira at 1992 Deep Space Nine press conference.

# CHARACTER PROFILE

# MAJOR KIRA NERYS

Kira Nerys is a Bajoran who grew up on a world where freedom was only a word and a memory. The Cardassians had invaded and conquered her world. Neither Bajor nor Cardassia were allied with the Federation and, consequently did not come under the rules governing the aligned worlds of the Federation. The Bajoran question was a dispute between two worlds which fell outside Starfleet jurisdiction.

Kira's childhood was one of terror and horror that quickly hardened her into a Bajoran terrorist. Kira was raised in the refugee camps on Bajor and has, in her own words, "been fighting the Cardassians since she was old enough to pick up a phaser."

Her hatred for the Cardassians caused her to join a terrorist group. She fought along with Tahna Los in the Bajoran underground known as the Shakaar. Kira took her involvement in the group seriously and was high offended when, after the liberation of Bajor, she found a Cardassian file which classified her as being a minor operative who ran errands for the Shakaar.

Though the Cardassian threat has been removed from her home world, she stil finds herself wrestling with the past. Beset by nightmares and plagued by guilt, coming to terms with her past has not been easy. After the liberation of Bajor, Kira was able to get some comfort from Kai Opaka. The religious leader convinced Kira that she must learn to accept the violence that is inside her because only then can she learn to live beyond it. Kira's major concern is that the Prophets won't forgive her for the violent life she led fighting the Cardassians. Kira gained strength from the words of the Kai and was surprised at Opaka's response—that the prophets were just waiting for her to forgive herself.

## Choosing Another Path

While the Cardas-sians considered any Bajor-ans who opposed them to be terrorists, Kira was a member of an active faction who set off bombs and assassinated collaborators. When she investigated a suspected collaborator aboard the mining platform called Deep Space Nine, she was caught by the man while searching his shop and was forced to kill him in self-defense. The Cardassians suspected that the man's murder was more than just a foiled robbery and set about finding his killer. Kira managed to elude suspicion by confessing to Odo that she was committing a different terrorist act at the time of the man's murder.

Kira rose to the rank of major in the Bajoran underground, a rank she retained even after she quit her cell because of disagreements about the faction's. She believed that Bajorans were better than their Cardassian overlords and stooping to using the methods of their conquerors was no solution. She agreed with attacking military targets, supply lines and other important conduits of commerce, but drew the line at murdering civilians just because they were Cardassians. She would later learn that her belief that not all Cardassians were alike was true, a realization that would both joy and grief.

One of her most difficult encounters with a Cardassian was when Kira helped to liberate the notorious forced labor camp known as Gallitepp. Thousands of Bajorans died there and the conditions at the camp left many Cardassians branded as war criminals. When she believed she had finally encountered one such criminal, it was all she could do to maintain her professional posture and not strangle the Cardassian.

Kira initially op-posed the invitation to join the Federation. She was concerned that the provisional Bajoran government was splinterring into petty factions. Over time, she came to recognize that only with the support of the Federation would Bajor be able to rebuild without the threat of Cardassian re-invasion.

## New Battles

Because Bajor was so effectively plundered by their former overlords, the Cardassians, they remain rich strategically while poor economically and are barely able to support their population. With Bajor now a world bent on rebuilding its fractured civilization, Major Kira accepts the fact that she will now be fighting red tape rather than Bajoran rights violations.

No sooner did the Federation arrive to oversee the refitting of the space station and the shipment of relief supplies to Bajor, than Major Kira was faced with a renewed

Nana Visitor.

Photo c 1994 Alvert L. Ortega

Nana Visitor at Universal Studios, November, 1993.

**Photo c 1994 Alvert L. Ortega**

attack by the Cardassians who were furious at giving up Bajor right before the wormhole was discovered. Suddenly that small world had become one of the most strategically important planets in the Alpha Quadrant in terms of commerce and the Bajorans came close to losing it again before they could even grow accustomed to the sensation of freedom.

Some of her former comrades in the old Bajoran underground regard her as a traitor for breaking ranks with them before the fight was over. That she chose to continue the fight on her own terms is of little consequence to them. She feels that some of the former terrorists are uncomfortable with their new lot in life now that freedom has been won. She believes that they are opposing the Federation merely because they need an enemy to justify their continued existence. What is a freedom fighter if they have nothing to fight?

Kira has seen the help the Federation and Starfleet can bring to Bajor and she is willing to oppose even her own people if it means taking the side of the Federation in order to protect the greater interests of Bajor against the fractional interests of those who cannot see the big picture.

## Duty and Principles

Major Kira is very impulsive and has risked her career for her principles on more than one occasion. She faced a delicate moral dilemma when a terrorist tried to enlist her aid against Bajor and the Federation. With Odo's guidance, she decided to tell Sisko the truth about the terrorist plan.

On another occasion, Kira refused to evict an old man named Mullibok from the Bajoran moon Jeraddo because he managed to deflect her confrontation by comparing what she was trying to do with what the Cardassians had done on Bajor. Eventually, she recognized that evicting the man was for the good of Bajor as the moon was needed for an energy project which

would help the people of Bajor through the coming winter. Taking personal responsibility, she set fire to Mullibok's home herself and ordered him evacuated and resettled.

She was relieved of her duties for a time when Li Nalas was given her post and she was reassigned back to the surface of Bajor. While on Bajor she encountered an orb at the monastery with Vedek Bareil and had a vision which led her and Dax to the Hall of ministers to expose the Cardassian plot to use the "Circle" to force out Starfleet. This happened after she escaped from the fundamentalist group that had been using Cardassian torture techniques on the Bajoran to force her to give up Starfleet's plans for supporting the provisional government.

Kira continues to struggle to fit in as she has finally found a place where she feels useful; a place where she belongs, even if she does complain that "Starfleet types" rely too much on "gadgets and gizmos."

## Dax and Julian

Kira has developed a close friendship with the Trill, often telling her secrets to Jadzia, trusting the symbiont to keep the secrets. Kira and Dax ventured to the Lunar Five colony where they appropriated a Bajoran rebel fighter and used it to get to Bajor. The two women survived the crash and were taken to the monastery of Vedek Bareil. Kira and Dax disguised themselves as Vedeks to enter the Hall of Ministers, there they exposed a Cardassian plot and prevented the "Circle" from gaining control of the Bajoran government.

Kira and Dax sometimes socialize while off duty, but one thing they do not have in common is their attitude regarding the Ferengi. Kira has never met a Ferengi she trusts and she finds Quark and his cronies to be particularly loathsome. On the other hand, Dax enjoys playing cards with the Ferengi and accepts their ill manners while finding them quite fascinating. When Kira found herself on the receiving end of the lascivious attentions of Zek, the Nagus, who would pinch her posterior without provocation, Kira remarked to herself, "Dax must be crazy."

Major Kira and the young doctor, Julian Bashir, got off on the wrong foot when he described her homeworld as the "frontier." She showed him a touch of her temper, but usually accepts his egotism with good humor. Julian felt great sadness for Kira at the death of Kai Opaka, much of it due to his inability to save her. Relief came, though, Opaka was restored by the people of planet Ennis.

## Odo and O'Brien

Odo is Kira's closest friend and most trusted companion. Kira first met the shape-shifter when Kira was falsely accused of having had an affair with a married man. Kira used Quark as an alibi, but that quickly fell apart when Odo threatened the Ferengi with a murder charge.

Kira admitted sabotaging the ore processing center and Odo was satisfied she didn't commit the crime. Odo had no suspect until years later when Kira, during the investigation of an attack on Quark, gave Odo a clue which indicated she knew more than she'd let on. Kira later admitted that she'd killed the Bajoran storekeeper in self-defense, yet held back the truth for five years since Odo was working for the Cardassians at the time. He asked why she had continued to hold back the information even after the Cardassians had pulled out. Kira explained that she didn't want to risk losing his trust and respect.

Odo and Kira are both outsiders and tend to do what they want, when they want to. They have short fuses and refuse to be tied down by regulations and red tape. The two form a perfect pair, yet each is still learning to fit in.

At first Miles O'Brien had little use for the Bajoran Major with her well-known disdain for Starfleet. However, as he found himself working closely with her, Miles began to realize just how committed she was to her duty. After Sisko became the "Emissary," her attitude changed markedly, but Miles did have a chance to "get back" at Kira when the crew was exposed to a telepathic signal that put Sisko and Miles in direct opposition to Dax, Kira and Julian. O'Brien and Kira made up when he volunteered to join her in the attempt to free Li Nalas from Cardassia IV. Miles survived a Cardassian massacre at Selik III and bore the mental scars inflicted by his deadly battle with the Cardassians. Both Miles and Kira have survived their run-ins with the Cardassians over the years, but each share anguish from the tragedies they were forced to witness.

## The Role of the Prophets

Although Kira isn't ordinarily expressive about it, she is a very religious individual and is more than willing to defend her religions and its leaders, the Vedeks and the Kai. When Vedek Winn challenged the teaching of scientific theories about the wormhole to Bajoran children while ignoring the religious significance of the Prophets, Major Kira defended the Vedek's point of view. She later came to realize that Vedek Winn was cynically manipulating her and the other Bajorans on the station for selfish purposes, but this does not shake Kira's religious faith.

Kai Opaka remains one of the most influential people in Kira's life. When their shuttle crashed on the planet Ennis and Opaka was killed, Kira sang a Bajoran death chant and was clearly shattered by the death of the Kai. When Opaka is miraculously resurrected Kira accepted it as a religious miracle, although she later learned that everyone who dies on Ennis is thereafter resurrected by the technology in orbit around that world. One of the most difficult things Kira had ever done was to leave Kai Opaka on Ennis and return to Bajor.

When Kira was shown an orb by Vedek Bareil which revealed a vision involving a future union with Bareil, Kira Nerys resisted the vision because it meant that she would have a physical relationship with one of the leaders of her religion. She wasn't certain she was ready for that as the Vedeks are regarded as being beyond the ordinary needs of the flesh. Although Kira has seen Vedek Bareil since her vision she has been unwilling to reveal what she saw, although it is evident that Bareil has experienced a similar vision when he looked into an orb. What this vision holds for Kira, Bareil and the future of Bajor remains to be seen.

# ACTOR PROFILE

# NANA VISITOR

The actress known as Nana Visitor was born in New York City on the west side. But due to her theatrical family she grew up in and around the theatre throughout her childhood. There in New York her mother was a ballet teacher in charge of a dance studio and her father was a Broadway choreographer on many successful musicals. In fact he had been a student of Nana's mother, which was how they met. Another one of her mother's early students was the now famous choreographer Tommy Tune.

By age seven Nana had begun studying ballet at the dance studio her mother ran, and by age 14 she was in her high school musicals. She made a crucial life decision when Nana had the opportunity to attend college at Princeton but turned it down in order to be a chorus girl in a stage musical. She never regretted the decision because she kept finding work at her chosen craft.

Soon the stage beckoned and Nana began appearing in productions of such plays as "Gypsy" (with Angela Lansbury), "My One And Only (where she worked with Tommy Tune)," "42nd Street," "A Musical Jubilee," and in Los Angeles at the Tiffany Theater she appeared in "The Ladies Room."

Before pursuing her acting career still further by moving to Los Angeles, she had regular roles on the soap operas RYAN'S HOPE and ONE LIFE TO LIVE. As a young actress she secured an early film role in the 1977 film THE SENTINEL, a horror movie filmed in New York City.

Nana VIsitor

**Photo c 1994 Alvert L. Ortega**

## Another Career Move

But finally she knew she'd have to move to Los Angeles if she wanted to find more film and TV work and she made the jump in 1985. When WORKING GIRL was briefly a TV series, Nana had the role of Bryn Newhouse, one of the main supporting characters. She also secured guest shots on such series as THIRTY SOMETHING, EMPTY NEST, MURDER SHE WROTE (in which she was reunited with Angela Lansbury, whom she had appeared with on stage in New York), MATLOCK, L.A. LAW, IN THE HEAT OF THE NIGHT, BABY TALK, and JAKE AND THE FATMAN.

In 1987 she starred opposite Sam Jones in the ill fated TV pilot of THE SPIRIT, based on a comic strip character. Nana played Ellen Dolan, a major supporting character in the storyline.

Nana admits that as a child she was a great STAR TREK fan, but as much as she liked the original series, she's glad that female characters are much more prominent on DEEP SPACE NINE than they ever were on either of the two previous STAR TREK series. She finds this a cause for celebration and a demonstration that DEEP SPACE NINE has its own identity and more possibilities for storylines than were possible on the other series. She readily admits that Major Kira is a revamped version of Ensign Ro Laren from THE NEXT GENERATION, but she feels that the two characters are different enough that she doesn't have to feel that she is living up to anyone's preconceived notion of how a Bajoran should look and act. Major Kira is her own person as she has proven more than once on DEEP SPACE NINE.

## A Moving Experience

Nana has explained that the only way she felt she could identify with the pain in Major Kira's life was due to her own experience in going through childbirth. "Freedom

fighter, nothing! Give birth!" She told SUPER-STAR FACTS magazine. "So I went out the morning [of the audition] and I got a pair of Doc Martens, and I put them on and felt like Major Kira. I felt like I'd just been through mud and rolled around and fought people and gotten a few Cardassians. Then I got there, I threw open the door, did two scenes, and left! I did the same thing for Paramount when I went back.

"I found out weeks later, when they got to know me, that they said, 'Well. . . she's really right for the role, but is she going to be a NIGHT-MARE? This is an unpleasant woman!' They didn't realize that this was Major Kira, and Major Kira just couldn't be bothered talking to people; she's going to do what she's got to do and she's out of there! So that's what I did!"

Visitor also admitted that the episode "Duet" wasn't just a powerful experience to watch, but to film as well. "My thought, every time I saw him, was that I was confronting pure evil, and I was confronting everything that's in the world today that hopefully won't be there in the 24th century. There were takes where I was bursting into tears, and I'd go to the director and say please, don't print that 'cause it was wrong for her to be in tears for the whole show. Very often I'd have to go somewhere and just get it all off. It was wrenching, and it was hard and Harris Yulin, our guest star, was wonderful."

Nana felt she got a great deal out of working on that episode. "Kira went through a lot and she had tremendous growth, and so did I. I used to turn off the TV when I saw civil wars or starvation and all the upsetting things in the world. Since that show, I watch. You can't turn it off; you can't pretend that it's not out there and that's the change that happened to me."

## On and Off the Set

The most difficult aspect of the series for her is the one and a half hour makeup session she must endure each morning and then the long hours spent at the studio. There have been times when she arrived at the studio at four o'clock in the afternoon and was still there working at two o'clock in the morning.

One amusing incident she relates involves the time she had completed hair and makeup when, still wearing her street clothes, she exited the makeup trailer and slipped and fell on rain slicked steps. Unable to move, she was taken to a doctor who did a double-take when he saw her nose until she explained that it was just makeup and she worked on STAR TREK.

As a person, Nana Visitor has dual careers as she is also a wife and mother. During the down time when she's not working on DEEP SPACE NINE she spends time with her husband, Nick and her child, who she calls Buster. After she'd been working on DS9 a few months she started bringing her baby to the studio with her so that she could spend more time with him. She enjoys going to STAR TREK conventions and meeting fans. Nana is perfectly willing to sign autographs and if it takes three hours for everyone to get an autograph, then she'll sign for three hours. And she's not interested in hurrying people along. She likes to meet them, look into their eyes and make a connection. To her the fans are what makes STAR TREK an enduring hit.

Nana used to watch the reruns of the original STAR TREK and she recalled working in Boston once on a play which never made it to Broadway and she discovered that there was a STAR TREK convention going on in town. "People were in costume and I thought what a great thing. It's like being in a club and you can go to any city and be a part of this wonderful thing. And I was jealous. I wanted in on this, but who knew? Who knew this would be the way I did it?"

Colm Meany in uniform at 1992 Deep Space Nine press conference. **Photo c 1994 Alvert L. Ortega**

# CHARACTER PROFILE

# MILES O'BRIEN

Coming from an artistic background, Miles father wanted him to be a musician. His father was heartbroken when Miles refused to accept a scholarship to become a musician at the Aldeberan Musical Academy. Miles instead ran away to join Starfleet Academy.

Miles O'Brien found that his winning ways and jovial personality often took him as far as did his seemingly innate talent for uncovering the problem in any mechanical device. He graduated fourth in his class from Starfleet Academy and was granted a deep space assignment as soon as he applied for it. This assignment was to a relatively small passenger liner. It was there that his skills with the transporter were sharpened, abilities that would serve him well in the years to come.

A shuttle service wasn't exactly what Miles anticipated being granted when he asked for a deep space assignment. There were greater challenges than that in Starfleet and he'd proved in the Academy that he was more than capable of meeting any challenge he encountered.

It was that skill for being a first rate troubleshooter that brought Miles to the attention of Ben Maxwell, Captain of the USS Rutledge, several years after O'Brien had graduated from Starfleet. He was transferred to the USS Rutledge. Captain Maxwell kept a sharp eye on his new technician and after several months of exemplary performance Miles was promoted to the rank of Bridge Tactical Officer, Lieutenant j.g. It was after this that Miles began to learn first-hand just how perilous a deep space assignment could be.

## The Dogs of War

When the Federation outpost on Setlik 3 was attacked by a Cardassian raiding party during the Federation's war with the Cardassians, the USS Rutledge was dispatched to help defend the outpost. But when the USS Rutledge arrived at Setlik 3 they were unable to communicate with the outpost on the planet below. O'Brien beamed down with the away team only to find that the outpost of more than one hundred people had been wiped out. The dead included the wife and children of Ben Maxwell.

But the Cardassians were still there, looting and pillaging the settlement. What the Rutledge had been unable to provide in assistance they tried to make up for in exacting vengeance. The fighting was brutal and during an encounter with two Cardassians, O'Brien was able to stun one but was forced to kill the other. In spite of the slaughter he had witnessed, killing was not an easy thing for him to do. He resented the Cardassians both for their crimes against humanity and for forcing him to kill in battle. That wasn't what he joined Starfleet to do. He carried a deep resentment for everything relating to Cardassians for years thereafter, and while he recognized the source of his prejudice he found it difficult to overcome.

It wasn't long before O'Brien's service distinctions warranted another promotion, this time to the rank of a full lieutenant. With it came a transfer to the Enterprise, the flagship of the Federation under the command of Captain Jean Luc Picard.

## Poker Face

On a ship so vast, O'Brien gained additional experience. He found his duties putting him at a variety of posts aboard ship, but it wasn't long before he had the permanent assignment as transporter chief, a post he served well.

As transporter chief, O'Brien seldom was assigned to the away teams the way he had been when he was posted to the Rutledge. Instead his skills were directed towards maintaining and operating the transporters. He was soon skilled at keeping the transporters functioning at their peak performance.

O'Brien had a reputation for being a shrewd card player and this led to an invitation to join the weekly poker game which some of the ship's officers indulged in. But Miles met his match in first officer Commander Riker. It wasn't unusual for the other players to fold just so they could sit back and observe the masters of the game at work. It made for an lively often evening.

It was apparently his recreational skills as much as anything else which dictated that O'Brien be selected to accompany Commander Riker on an away team mission to Alphard V, a world where

Colm Meany at premier of The Snapper.

gambling had been elevated to a high art. Their mission was not an elaborate shore leave but rather an investigation. Eighteen Federation personnel, including Captain Dale Robbins of Starfleet, had vanished on that deceptively harmless world. No trace of them had been found.

## Under Cover

Disguised as Federation tourists out to try their luck on the notorious gambling world, O'Brien, Riker, Worf and Troi beamed down along with two security guards to cover their backs. The guise of a wealthy group looking to drop a wad in the casinos seemed like a surefire lure for whoever had kidnapped the missing personnel.

Miles was up to the pose, gambling his time away with credits supplied by the Federation in the company of a comely lady Enterprise security guard, Ensign Jardenaux. As it turned out, O'Brien was the pigeon selected to be the next target. He and the ensign were beamed aboard an alien vessel, but a malfunctioning transporter caused them to materialize several feet above the floor. During the confusion that followed, O'Brien activated his communicator which notified the others as to where he was. As a result O'Brien saved his own life and that of his companions, as well as those of the other prisoners.

When they returned to the Enterprise, O'Brien chanced to ask Will Riker why he had selected him as part of the mission. The first officer admitted that it was because O'Brien looked the part and as it turned out he did indeed act his role well. So well in fact that Riker recommended that a commendation be placed in O'Brien's file. This could only have helped him when the time came to consider promotions.

Miles once had a fear of spiders until he was forced to climb into a tube full of the creatures to keep a generator from being destroyed. Miles later took an alien tarantula as a pet as a way to further overcome that fear.

## Past Prologue

When Ben Maxwell, O'Brien's old commander, suffered a breakdown and began attacking Cardassian vessels because he believed that his former enemies were rearming for war, Captain Picard called on Miles to convince his former captain to surrender his starship, the USS Phoenix. Maxwell was seeking revenge on the Cardassians as a race, blaming them all for the death of his family a few years before. Miles used his transporter skill to beam through a variance in the USS Phoenix's shield, allowing him to get to his former captain and reason with him. Miles used an old drinking song to get Maxwell to remember their old bond.

The quote he used was from philosopher Thomas Moore (1779-1852). The poem became a drinking song for warriors over the centuries. The poem was entitled "The Minstrel Boy."

*"The Minstrel boy to the war is gone,*
*In the ranks of death you'll find him;*
*His father's sword he has girded on,*
*And his wild harp slung behind him."*

O'Brien finally found the right woman in his life when he met Keiko Ishikawa, the botanist on the Enterprise. They eventually tied the knot with Geordi as best man. Data stood in for the father of the bride while Captain Picard performed the ceremony. Held in Ten Forward, it was an Irish/Japanese ceremony. Some months later Keiko gave birth to a little girl named Molly, with Worf acting as reluctant midwife.

O'Brien almost saw his future chances at promotion, much less existence, end when the Enterprise arrived at one of the moons of Mab-Bu VI. He was part of an away team, along with Data, Troi and Riker, and found his body taken over by an alien entity. Data and Troi also suffered this fate as beings who had been trapped on

Colm Meany

Photo c 1994 Alvert L. Ortega

that world, actually imprisoned there, saw their one chance to escape. It was through the efforts of Captain Picard, Riker and others that the plot of the aliens was defeated and they were forced to vacate the bodies they had stolen. Through a fluke, the being in O'Brien's body found himself with a group of hostages that included Keiko and her baby. But O'Brien was himself in form only and threatened his wife along with the other hostages, a nightmarish circumstance which it took Keiko some time to get over.

## The Far Frontier

When the time came around for promotions, Miles found himself offered the opportunity to transfer to Deep Space Nine, a former mining station in orbit around Bajor. The Cardassians had just abandoned that world and the Bajorans had appealed to the Federation for assistance. Miles was to be posted as Chief Operations officer on the space station, a role that would prove to be grueling and difficult due to the condition the Cardassians had left the station in. O'Brien had wanted deep space assignments, and following 22 years spent on starships he was posted to this solitary site in the Alpha Quadrant, a space station well named for its remoteness. Keiko and Molly accompanied him, but his wife wasn't as prepared for what she found as she thought she'd be.

Keiko quickly found that this new life was far different from what she'd known aboard the Enterprise. A botanist was like a fifth wheel aboard the space station and she chaffed under the conditions of her new lifestyle. She and Miles often argued and Miles wondered if his marriage would stand up to the strain. But finally Keiko solved the problem herself by establishing a school on the station for the children who lived on Deep Space Nine. This was something that made her feel useful again and the happiness returned to Miles and Keiko's marriage.

Other things have plagued Miles, though, such as when his mother died shortly before his posting to Deep Space Nine. The fact that his father remarried in less than a year troubled him greatly as he felt it somehow dishonored his mother's memory to remarry so soon.

## Face to Face

After being on the station for about a year, O'Brien was on a mission to Baradas when he was captured by a government group. They replaced Miles on the station with a replicant, but not even the replicant knew he wasn't the real Miles O'Brien. The government wanted to disrupt the peace conference which was designed to end twelve years of civil war. The alternate Miles realized he was being cut out of the loop of command on the station and began to believe that Sisko, Kira, Keiko, Odo and all the others had been replaced or in some other way changed.

Finally the real Miles was freed by rebel groups who contacted Sisko and warned of the planned replicant. The cloned being actually believed he was Miles O'Brien and had all of his memories that had been transferred from sensors which read the brain waves of the real Miles O'Brien.

In a way, that duplicate Miles was just as real as the William "Thomas" Riker that had been created in a transporter mishap. That alternate Riker (who is now serving as a lieutenant on the USS Ghandi) has none of the memories of Will's future events since that day on the USS Potemkin when one Will beamed back to the ship while the other was forced to accept that he would have to work to catch up with his "twin." In sharp contrast, this Miles had every memory that the real Miles possessed. His death was tragic, to none as much as Miles, who is left with the personal logs "He" made while that other Miles tried to unravel the mystery of what was going on.

## The Odd Couple

Miles once returned to Earth with Keiko to visit her mother in Komomoto, but the next time Keiko visited Earth she went alone. Julian has mentioned gossip implying that the O'Brien's marriage is less than ideal, a suggestion that Miles is quick to take offense at.

Miles and Julian have been paired off on assignments more than once, something that O'Brien was initially against as he found Dr. Bashir annoying. But the two have developed a genuine mutual respect. Miles and Julian's banter is laced with sarcasm on Miles' part, torn between liking Julian as a friend and equating him with a "fresh out of Starfleet Academy" tenderfoot. Miles just rolls his eyes as Julian tries to win over Bajoran women with his tales of Starfleet Medical finals. (For instance, a misidentification of pre-gangliatic fiber caused Julian to finish second, "The stuff salutatorians are made of," Julian gushed.)

Miles has two brothers, a wife, Keiko, daughter Molly Worf Ishikawa O'Brien, as well as his father, step-mother and his centurian mother-in-law in Japan.

Colm Meany.

Photo c 1994 Alvert L. Ortega

# ACTOR PROFILE
# COLM MEANEY

A native of Great Britain, Colm (pronounced "column") was born in Dublin, Ireland. As a youth he was intrigued by acting and began to pursue it in earnest when he was fourteen.

After his high school graduation he applied for admission to the National Irish Theater drama school. Colm worked on a fishing boat while awaiting word on his acceptance, but as soon as he received word that the school would admit him, he left the world of fishing behind.

For eight years the young actor worked in such British theatrical productions as "Accidental Death of an Anarchist" and, ironically enough considering his recent employment, "Fish in the Sea."

His TV debut was in a then popular police series called "Z CARS" (pronounced Zed Cars as the letter "Z" is pronounced "zed" in England). He also appeared in the film STRANGERS and then made the big decision to move to the United States in 1978.

## An Intercontinental Performer

For the next four years he hop-scotched back and forth between New York and London as he played a number of roles in films, television and on-stage. In 1982 he decided to remain in America permanently to concentrate his professional efforts here. For the next few years he primarily did stage work in regional theater and off-Broadway before making another move, this time from New York to Los Angeles. This enabled him to do more regular auditions for TV and movie roles.

The roles came his way and he made guest shots on such shows as TALES FROM THE DARK SIDE, REMINGTON STEELE, and MOONLIGHTING. Initially he was cast in the tough guy roles playing menacing characters, but he enjoyed the change of pace when he landed the role of Chief O'Brien, who would become an irregular regular, on STAR TREK—THE NEXT GENERA-TION, appearing in some 60 episodes. When he ini-tially auditioned for the series he not only had never seen any version of STAR TREK, he wasn't even a science fiction fan. He originally auditioned for some of the other roles, including Data, but ulti-mately was cast as the Enterprise transporter chief, who at the time did-n't even have a name. Meaney appeared in the very first episode of NEXT GENERATION, "Encounter At Farpoint," and then made infrequent appearances over the next two years before the pro-ducers decided to start beefing up his character to make him more than just a glorified extra.

While working on those early seasons of NEXT GENERATION, Colm often did other work as since it didn't look like his role on the show would ever develop into anything substantial. Following the first three episodes of TNG in 1987, Colm flew back to New York and appeared for nine months in the play "Breaking the Code" with Derek Jacobi. When the play closed after a year, NEXT GENERATION was on hiatus due to the Writer's Guild Strike, so Colm remained in New York and landed a role on the daytime drama ONE LIFE TO LIVE. This role lasted until the fall of 1988, when the Hollywood Writer's Guild strike ended.

## Recalled to Duty

Paramount then summoned Colm Meaney back to the studio where the character of the transporter chief was given a name, Chief O'Brien, and more lines as the first stage in developing his character. He appeared in seventeen episodes in the second season of NEXT GENERATION. One of his early featured episodes was the second season outing "Unnatural Selection" in which Chief O'Brien had to call upon his transporter skills in order to save the ship's Chief Surgeon, Dr. Pulaski, from an ailment which had brought about rapid aging.

Unlike most of the other cast members of STAR TREK—THE NEXT GENERATION, Colm Meaney has a number of motion picture credits. These include roles in such films as COME SEE THE PARADISE, DICK TRACY, DIE HARD II: DIE HARDER, THE LAST OF THE MOHICANS, FAR AND AWAY (where he coached star Tom Cruise on his accent), THE COMMITMENTS and UNDER SIEGE. He also appeared in the TV movie THE GAMBLER III. He even appeared in the pilot episode of DR. QUINN, MEDICINE WOMAN but didn't join the subsequent series because of his commitment to DEEP SPACE NINE. He also appeared in the pilot for EQUAL JUSTICE and in the HBO movie PERFECT WITNESS.

In the fourth season episode "Family" he was officially revealed to be Miles Edward O'Brien instead of just Chief O'Brien. Also in the fourth season, O'Brien was featured prominently in "The Wounded" when Captain Picard had him talk to his former captain who had turned renegade and was attacking all Cardassian vessels. It made for a good character scene for the performer as he revealed how he, too, had lost friends at the hands of the Cardassians during the war with them.

## Call Me Slasher!

Meaney has often had to play villains and while his STAR TREK persona is a very benevolent one, in the fifth season episode "Power Play" the character of Chief O'Brien was possessed by a dangerous alien entity, along with Troi and Data. Behind the scenes the three actors had names for their evil selves which were never revealed on air. Brent Spiner was dubbed Buzz, Marina took the nom de plum of Slugger, and Colm called himself Slasher.

Another interesting episode for Meaney was "Rascals" in which Keiko is transformed into a child due to a transporter accident. The young actress, Caroline Junko King, who played the adolescent Keiko had appeared in COME SEE THE PAR-ADISE, a film Meaney had also appeared in.

When Berman and Piller were developing their STAR TREK spin-off DEEP SPACE NINE, they decided that Miles O'Brien would be the perfect NEXT GENERATION character to make the transition to the new series, which would otherwise be popu-lated with entirely new characters. After all, Miles had married Keiko (Rosalind Chao) and had a daughter, Molly, so they had a ready made family to transfer to the space sta-tion. This also enabled Colm Meaney to become one of the first team of ensemble performers rather than being part of the second string of sup-porting characters such as he'd been on NEXT GEN-ERATION.

In a talk with COMICS INTERVIEW magazine, Meaney explained the advantages in the way his character was shaped on THE NEXT GENERA-TION. "The character was developed over a long peri-od, about four years, and that really helps an actor.

You're not suddenly faced with a whole new agenda or anything, it's a gradual process and that's always easier to deal with than suddenly trying to create a whole new thing. And the transition from NEXT GENERATION to DEEP SPACE NINE was easier because they were writing more and more for me on NEXT GENERATION; there were a few episodes where they developed O'Brien further. It feels like a logical continuation of what I was doing on NEXT GENERATION, really, the way we've moved him onto the space station."

## In a Family Way

Colm was particularly pleased that Rosalind Chao was willing to do the series because this enabled them to play the kind of character situations seldom seen on science fiction shows. "Keiko, Miles and Molly are the only family we see in space," Meaney explained. "I love the shows where Rosalind is involved and we get to play family situations. The one thing that SF shows tend to lack is simple, real family business, like making a cup of tea or having dinner. There's usually no time for that on TV shows. Interpersonal relationships and the like don't get much air time on SF shows, either. Having Keiko and Molly there gives me more aspects of my character to explore. That's a tremendous plus."

Family relationships are clearly important to Colm for it was after he relocated to the United States that he started his own family when he married his wife, Barbara, and had a daughter named Brenda, who is now eight years old. When Colm appeared with the other DEEP SPACE NINE cast members at Universal Studios Hollywood in November 1993, his daughter was in the audience and he proudly introduced her to the assembled fans.

In spite of working on a weekly series, Colm has been able to continue working in motion pictures as 1993 saw him appear in two British films: INTO THE WEST and

SNAPPER. SNAPPER was filmed in Ireland and was directed by Stephen Frears. It is a sequel to THE COMMITMENTS although it is not about the Irish rock band. Meaney played the father of the main character in THE COMMITMENTS and SNAPPER tells the story of the father and his oldest daughter (not seen in the previous film). Regarding the difficulties of working on a series while still fielding feature film offers, Meaney explains that the producers have been very accomodating to him. "This film I just did was in Ireland and they worked out the dates and said, 'Yeah, we can make that work,' and released me to go do it. It gives you the best of both worlds when you can do the series while, at the same time, occasionally get out to do something different."

Colm Meaney has come a long way since he first moved to the United States in 1978 and two STAR TREK series have been all the better for his presence.

# CHARACTER PROFILE
# KEIKO O'BRIEN

Although she does not appear in every episode of STAR TREK: DEEP SPACE NINE, Keiko O'Brien is a crucial part of the cast of characters— especially where Chief O'Brien is concerned. Keiko met and married Miles O'Brien while the both were stationed on board the Enterprise under the command of Jean-Luc Picard. Their relationship has always been troubled. At one point, Keiko actually called off the wedding, frustrating both O'Brien and the observing android, Data.

However, they loved each other deeply, as they do to this day, and soon had a child. Their daughter Molly was born during a disaster that left Keiko stranded in Ten Forward. She gave birth aided by a very unlikely midwife: the Klingon Worf! (Worf had actually studied this procedure in a computer simulation, but found the real life experience to be somewhat more challenging.)

Trials and tribulations continued to assail their relationship. A strange alien influence that deprived the Enterprise crew of sleep drove Miles to paranoid delusions that Keiko was cheating on him. Later, when Miles was taken over by a malicious alien entity, he actually threatened his own wife and child with violence. Turnabout may be fair play, but Miles O'Brien was in for a strange experience when Keiko was temporarily transformed, as the result of a very strange accident, into a little girl of about twelve. Small wonder they wanted to get off the Enterprise.

Rosalind Chao.                    Photo c 1994 Alvert L. Ortega

## A CHANGE OF LIFE

Unfortunately, the challenging assignment O'Brien chose was as the Chief of Operations in the forbidding metal corridors of Deep Space Nine, where Keiko reluctantly joined him. She did not feel that the shadowy station is the place to raise a child, but agreed because she wants the family to stay together. This is yet another source of friction in their marriage. There is not much use for a botanist on a station where most, if not all, of the plant life is found in simulations in Quark's Holosuites. But Keiko was determined to make a place for herself on the station.

Seeing that the handful of children on the station lacked anything to do, Keiko decided to create a school. She met with some opposition from some locals, notably Quark, who felt that his nephew Nog should learn only Ferengi teachings and the Rules of Acquisition. Fortunately, she was able to convince him that knowledge of alien ways would only be more profitable for the boy in the long run. Even though Nog was pulled out of the school when the Ferengi Grand Nagus, Zek, paid a visit to the station, Keiko kept her commitment to the school.

Keiko does leave the station temporarily, however, traveling to Earth to visit her one-hundred-year old mother. When she returns, her relationship with Miles seems more relaxed. The episode "If Wishes Were Horses" opens with the Miles and Keiko spending a pleasant evening at home after tucking in their daughter Molly, who has just greatly enjoyed a reading of the classic fairy tale of Rumplestiltskin.

However, the bizarre troubles that have beset this marriage do not let up. When little Molly O'Brien claims to have seen the famous storybook dwarf, the happy parents are amused—until it turns out that Rumplestiltskin, or something appearing and acting just like him, has actually appeared in their daughter's room. Similar events plague the station.

At first it appeared that a highly destructive rift in space, the Hanoli rift, is linked to all these goings-on. Actually, Rumple-stilt-skin and the other beings on the station created the illusion of a planet-threatening rift. These beings are from beyond the Gamma Quadrant and were exploring in their own fashion. Having this "imaginary" Rumplestiltskin trying to claim their daughter was just another bizarre space stress for Keiko O'Brien!

## THE BAJORAN CHALLENGE

Keiko soon faces a much more concrete adversary when the fundamentalist Bajoran religious leader Vedek Winn comes to the Deep Space Nine school room and politely but firmly asserts that Keiko's teaching of alien viewpoints is blasphemous to Bajoran eyes, at least to Bajoran eyes as narrow in their views as those of Vedek Winn. Keiko faces a battle of wills and philosophies. All she wants to teach is pure science, but even Kira Nerys thinks that two schools—one for Bajorans, another for the rest of the races on Deep Space Nine— would be more appropriate.

Vedek Winn even makes veiled threats against the school to Sisko indicating that Keiko, "has dishonored the celestial temple." Soon, most of the Bajorans on the station are giving Keiko and Miles O'Brien the cold shoulder, refusing even to sell them vegetables. Spurred on by Vedek Winn, who assumes a very rational mode of discourse but who is clearly a reactionary bigot, the Bajoran parents on Deep Space Nine form a crowd at the school and remove their children. It is obvious, however, that some are bowing to the pressure of Winn and her followers among their peers.

As if this was not enough, an explosion rocks the empty school room the next day. Keiko's little project is far more controversial than she could ever imagined. Determined to see it through, she puts things back together and proceeds

to teach to the few students who can and will still come. It later becomes apparent that the school issue was really a ploy to lure another, more moderate Bajoran cleric to the station and attempt to assassinate him. However, Keiko is now, more than ever, dedicated to the school.

## A FAMILY PERSON

Keiko's marriage is clearly subjected to a remarkably unusual amount of stress on Deep Space Nine. When Miles leaves on a dangerous mission to rescue a Bajoran prisoner of war from the Cardassians, Keiko was not even consulted. But she is a strong-willed and resourceful woman who will do everything she can do to keep her family and marriage together. With a little help from Miles O'Brien, she should be able to pull it off without a hitch.

Life for the pair get even more strange when Miles is kidnapped and replaced by a replicant and

Keiko is instructed not to say or do anything to indicate that she knows the truth. The twist is that the replicant believes that it is real, that it is actually Miles, and thinks that something is wrong with Keiko. It even professes its love for Keiko as it lays dying.

Between replicants and racquetball games which tax Miles' skills, Keiko remains the supportive wife and mother; she is certainly a very different from take-charge career women like Major Kira and Jadzia Dax. Although Keiko's life is less colorful than that of Dax and Kira, she is no less important. She is a wife and mother, roles that neither Dax nor Kira have at this time. Clearly Keiko wants to be more than wife and mother and it seems that, for now, being a teacher fulfills her need to feel that she has a useful role at the station.

Rosalind Chao.

Photo c 1994 Alvert L. Ortega

# ACTOR PROFILE

# ROSALIND CHAO

Rosalind Chao has been working in television for many years; her appearances can be traced as far back as KUNG FU in the early 70's. She appeared in the final episode of M*A*S*H as the Korean woman whom Klinger marries and, in more recent years, she was seen on the TV series BEAUTY AND THE BEAST.

The character of Keiko was introduced on STAR TREK—THE NEXT GENERA-TION and appeared in the episodes "The Wounded," "Power Play," "In Theory," "Rascals," and "Night Terrors." In the TNG episode "Data's Day" her character married Miles O'Brien and in "Disaster" Keiko gave birth to their child. Her appearances on DEEP SPACE NINE were infrequent furing the first season but have increased in the second season.

Colm Meany has only praise for his DEEP SPACE NINE co-star. "It's funny, Rosalind and I had an immediate rapport when we started on NEXT GENERATION. When we were getting married on NEXT GENERATION, her real-life husband, Simon Templeman, was actually working on a play in Costa Mesa with my wife, Barbara. It was very strange. My wife would go to work with Simon and I would come here to work with Roz. We had a lot in common: Rosalind is married, I'm married; Rosalind recently had a baby. I have a child. She's great to work with. There really wasn't much time to develop a relationship, to sit at a table and rehearse. We just seemed to click from the beginning."

Siddig el Fadil in uniform at 1992 Deep Space Nine press conference. **Photo c 1994 Alvert L. Ortega**

# DOCTOR JULIAN BASHIR

An incident that occurred when he was just ten years old propelled young Julian Bashir into a life of medicine. Although he didn't realize it at the time and wouldn't for years to come, that incident on a lonely desolate planetoid would shape his destiny.

Julian was a typical ten year old, scared out of his wits as he and his father struggled to survive an ionic storm on Ivernia II. He and his father were lost in the storm when they happened upon a young Ivernian girl who was dying. Bashir's father, a Federation diplomat, went to get medical help, but he was too late. The girl died.

To his horror Julian learned that a common herb, readily available and growing nearby, would have saved that child's life: he could have saved her if only he had the knowledge. This one event influenced Julian's decision to choose medicine over all the other career opportunities available to the young student.

## Searching for Answers

Julian was a very sociable child, unlike many children whose intellect is near the genius level. While growing up he tended to choose his friends from among the children of professional people.

When he would visit someone's home in the company of his father, young Julian would slip off to his host's library and begin exploring whatever medical or science books he could find. The boy would find a quiet corner and work unseen while his hosts discussed some momentous question in their respective technical fields of expertise.

That Julian so indulged himself, albeit quietly and unobtrusively, was revealed when his father and a doctor friend were discussing a medical breakthrough, about which Julian had recently been reading. In his eagerness to learn more and be a part of all this, Julian slipped up behind the doctors and began asking a series of technical questions about the new procedure.

While the physicians were initially annoyed and skeptical about the boy's behavior, they quickly became impressed that a ten year old could acquire so much knowledge. Young Julian was rewarded for his enthusiasms by being allowed to sit in on some of their informal gatherings. Actually, Julian admitted that they did not invite him so much as they allowed him to remain when he sat down with them, so long as he didn't become too intrusive. To make up for this he would take careful notes and look up the answers to his questions later.

## Modern Medicine

Julian was always interested in sports. When he was twelve, one of his friends was hurt during a ballgame and it was then that Julian had an opportunity to witness the complicated inner workings of a hospital. He entered the medical center with his friend and soon found himself distracted by everything he saw, from the smell of the sterilized facilities to the variety of equipment.

When his friend was admitted, he and his companions were required to stay in the waiting room. While there, Julian offered comfort to a couple who brought in their sick baby by pointing out how efficient the staff was and how up to date the equipment. Julian was so impressed by what he had seen at the hospital that he began to visit the medical center whenever he could, in spite of the best efforts of the medical staff to shoo him away. However, the hospital was as important to young Julian Bashir as was eating and breathing.

Finally he was allowed to perform small tasks such as keeping the waiting room neat and orderly and getting drinks for visitors. Because he made certain that he did not get in the way of the doctors and orderlies, Julian was not only tolerated but also given increasingly more freedom.

Siddig el Fadil and Colm Meany.

## A Matter of Life and Death

The turning point occured when a freak explosion in the city suddenly caused the emergency room to be flooded with patients. After listening helplessly as a doctor called for a nurse when none were available, Julian stepped forward uncertainly, expecting to be brutally rejected, and offered to help. The doctor paused for just a second and then told him to get scrubbed and back at his side as quickly as possible. Death and terror was in the air and lives hung in the balance.

Minutes later Julian was standing silently at the doctor's side, looking up at him as the physician asked for instruments whose names the boy had learned long ago. When a patient had been stabilized, the boy helped push the gurney out of the operating theater so that the next one could be rolled in. He wiped sweat from the faces of the hard-working doctors until everyone took him for granted. What Julian could not take for granted, however, was the act of pulling the sheet over the face of a young girl who had been too badly hurt to be saved..

Six hours later an exhausted boy sat silently in the staff lounge, thinking about all that he had seen and done that day. The doctor who had first put Julian to work walked in and looked down at the boy wearing the now blood spattered green surgery gown. He sat down next to Julian and gently thanked him, pointing out that he firmly believed that two of the patients on whom he had worked would not have survived without Julian's assistance. He thanked the boy and told him never to give up his dream of being a doctor.

## New Horizons

Julian thanked him and tried to smile; even though the doctor said that he had help save two people who might otherwise have died, he could not stop thinking of the little girl who was not so fortunate. She reminded him of that other little girl who had died before his eyes. This time he knew that nothing could have saved the girl, but he hated the thought that death could so quickly snatch away the life of one so young—younger even than himself.

Although medicine had been his dream since he was ten years old, when he was a teenager his parents took him on a tour of other planets; this tour marked yet another turning point in his young life. Seeing all that the galaxy had to offer made him more aware than ever before of the possibilities the future held. The stars called to him and he knew that he could accomplish more out in the galaxy than he could by remaining on Earth.

One of the most interesting facets of this journey had been all of the aliens he saw, broadening the possibilities in space medicine. When he applied to Starfleet Medical, Julian knew that one of his specialties in space medicine would be alien lifeforms. In fact he did not wait to see what Starfleet would teach him but once again dove into an intensive course of study and research on his own.

## The Lure of Starfleet

While in Paris, Julian met and fell in love with a ballerina whom he intended to marry. His soon-to-be-father-in-law offered him a job at a Parisian hospital but Julian turned down the job because he was determined to go to Starfleet Medical. This ended the relationship with both the ballerina and her family. Years later he would express regret over this and wonder whether he could have somehow had a wife and a career had he taken different turns in his life.

Some very illustrious people had written authoritative texts on xenobiology: for instance, Zephram Cochran, inventor of the warp drive. Cochran had an extended lifespan due to an alien being. He became an expert in the field of space medicine as it applied to non-humanoid lifeforms. Of course there was Leonard McCoy, a legend in Starfleet by the time Julian Bashir entered his official years of training at Starfleet Medical. Vulcan physiology was also an

Siddig el Fadil.

Photo c 1994 Alvert L. Ortega

important course of study and included a class taught by Commander Selar, who served for a time on the Enterprise under Jean-Luc Picard.

Julian spent eight years in Starfleet Medical to insure that he was as prepared as possible to practice medicine. Somehow he was able to complete his studies with high grades while not neglecting a secondary interest—the opposite sex.

## A Failure to Communicate

Julian loved women and women, in turn, were drawn to his dark good looks with equal enthusiasm. Though he was charming, he lacked one important trait: he didn't know how to talk to women. Unless they were medical students like himself he would bewilder them with a maze of technobabble. This problem still plagued him even after he completed school and was posted to Deep Space Nine. He talked at length about how he finished second in his class only by missing one question concerning a misidentification of pre-gangliatic fiber. "The stuff salutatorians are made of," he would explain as his date's eyes glazed over. It took some big brotherly advice from Miles O'Brien to finally get Julian to see the obvious.

Julian did indeed graduate from Starfleet Medical second in his class and this position meant that he would have a better opportunity to be posted exactly where he wanted to go— the furthest frontier of the Federation where anything was possible. After he arrived at the space station called Deep Space Nine some people misunderstood his enthusiasm as naiveté. Julian's enthusiasm was simply a love of adventure; and, for him, practicing space medicine at the edge of the galactic frontier was the height of adventure.

Julian was determined to be the best doctor possible and so was troubled by state of the Deep Space Nine sickbay. The Cardassians had left the sickbay in disrepair and

Julian constantly requested equipment and material to update the medical facilities.

## The Unreachable Dax

After arriving on the space station, Julian began pursuing the lovely science officer, Jadzia Dax. That she is a Trill containing a several-hundred -year-old symbiont did give him pause, but the exterior of Dax that most intrigued him. After months of platonic meetings and polite rebuffs, Julian finally got the message and began directing his attentions elsewhere.

Although Dr. Bashir and Miles O'Brien did not initially hit it off, they have managed to develop a respect and understanding for each other and have even played racquetball together. They had a spirited series of matches before Quark, using a charity benefiting Bajoran war orphans to entice the two, tricked them into playing a grudge match. Quark billed it as Miles "The Mechanic" O'Brien vs.

Julian "The Doctor" Bashir. The match was going in O'Brien's favor when he smashed the video monitor and realized that the laws of probability had somehow been scrambled up in his favor, both in the game room and on the rest of the station as well. The match was halted in order to investigate this phenomenon further and ferret out the truth.

Julian and Miles were officially reported as dead when they vanished during an attempt to destroy a deadly biogenic weapon. The two had been targeted for death, along with all the scientists who had knowledge of the deadly "Harvesters" virus. Miles was infected with the plague, forcing him to bond with Julian. They waited together for a seemingly impossible rescue, which somehow arrived in time.

## The Woman Who Could Fly

Bashir had an unusual romance on Deep Space Nine with an Elasian

Starfleet officer, Ensign Melora Pazlar. Melora arrived on board the USS Yellowstone on Stardate 47229.1 to do a series of studies in the Gamma Quadrant. Elasia is a low surface gravity world so Melora is one of the few Elasians to ever leave home. She must sit in a special chair and use a low-grav field actuator which allows her to overcome the station's artificial gravity.

Julian falls in love with Melora as he helps her adapt to the station, taking her out for Klingon food and sampling other delicacies. She surprises him in the Klingon restaurant because instead of being repulsed by the Klingon "gagh," she instead berates the amused chef for serving up half-dead mealworms. She is attracted enough to Julian to allow him into her private micro-gravity room where the two dance in the air.

Melora later asks Dax about the advisability of an interspecies romance. Dax notes that it has been 150 years since romance worked for the symbiont, but she inspired Melora with the tale of a hydrogen-breathing Lothra who fell in love with an Oxygene. They were together for 57 years despite being limited to 40 minutes a day contact without breathing apparatus.

## A Crucial Decision

Julian used neurostimulator therapy developed by Nathaniel Tarros for neuro-muscular adaptation. It was with this therapy that Melora was able to overcome Falat Kot. Shot with a phaser set to kill, the neurostimulators protected Melora. She knocked out the gravity generator and overpowered the murderer who had come to kill Quark.

In spite of how skillfully Dr. Bashir had managed to work his technological marvels on Melora, she decided to stop the treatments. Their ultimate success would prevent her from returning to her home planet to fly among her friends and family. She preferred the chair to losing her own identity as an

Elasian. She pointed out that Julian would still be able to publish a paper on his work applying Tarros' research from 30 years before to combine the neurostimulators with the neo-eleptic transmitters. This inspired application allowed for neuro-muscular increases in tensile strength, thereby allowing the body to support itself in gravity much higher than Elasian physiognomy would normally permit.

Julian arrived at the frontier outpost called Deep Space Nine searching for adventure. His fellow officers at first mistrusted this adventure-seeking, but they have come to recognize that Dr. Bashir is truly one of the most skilled doctors Starfleet has ever produced and that Julian is a fast friend as well.

—*Kay Doty and Alex Burleson*

Siddig el Fadil promoting the Deep Space Nine comic book.

**Photo c 1994 Alvert L. Ortega**

# ACTOR PROFILE

# SIDDIG EL FADIL

Siddig el Fadil was born in Sudan, Africa; his mother is English and his father, Sudanese. When Siddig was just a year old his family moved to England. He then grew up in England, attending public school and going on to the London University College for a year.

Early on, Siddig knew that he wanted to be in the theater, but acting was not his first calling: Siddig wanted to be a director. This urge gnawed at him for two years while he worked in a men's clothing store. Finally he had to make a decision. He quit his job and went to acting school. Although he wanted to be a director, he believed that he needed to understand the work of an actor in order to direct and get a peak performance out of actors.

After enrolling in the London Academy of Music and Dramatic Arts he found his acting classes thrusting him into productions of such plays as "Arthur" as well as Shakespeare's "Hamlet." He attended the London Academy of Music and Dramatic Arts for three years and upon graduation he was accepted into the company of the Manchester Library Theater in London. While there he had minor roles in their productions of "Sinbad the Sailor" and "Brother Eichemann."

Acting had never been his first calling, and tiring of being cast in minor roles, Siddig quit the theater company, believing that acting was just a dead end for him. He wanted to direct.

The Arts Threshold Theatre finally gave him the opportunity he had been working towards, giving him the helm of their production of the plays "Julius Caesar" and "Lotus and the Rats." It was while he was working at the Arts Threshold Theatre in the role of director that he was offered an acting role in a six part television mini-series called BIG BATTAL-IONS. In 1991 Siddig made his TV debut in the role of a Palestinian. He was so well received in this role that he was cast in another television production titled A DANGER-OUS MAN—LAWRENCE AFTER ARABIA as King Faisel.

## The PBS Connection

Although the role of King Faisel was relatively minor, when the program was aired on the Los Angeles PBS station the co-executive producer of DEEP SPACE NINE, Rick Berman and Piller were impressed by Siddig's performance. Siddig was originally considered for the role of Commander Ben Sisko, a character who was not written to be any specific race or ethnicity but considered to be fortyish. Berman and Piller did not realize that Siddig as King Faisel was actually a much younger actor playing an older role. After representatives of Paramount contacted Siddig in England, they informed Berman and Piller that Siddig El Fadil was just twenty-four—too young to be a middle-aged Starfleet career officer.

Initially Siddig did not realize what Berman and Piller had in mind. "I actually thought I was trying out for a guest spot on an episode because I had asked my agent to get me a spot on STAR TREK about a year ago. It was really after I auditioned for the Paramount executives that I realized it probably was not a guest spot. It was very exciting to find out that I was auditioning was for a regular on a series." Just days after his audition the actor found himself in Hollywood

Berman and Piller had been so impressed with Siddig that they wanted to test him for one of the other unfilled slots in the cast. They had him read for the role of Julian Bashir, the young, inexperienced medical officer who had joined Starfleet in search of adventure and opportunity.

## Meeting the Americans

Although Berman and Piller had not originally envisioned a medical officer with a British accent, they were won over by Siddig's ability and charm and decided that he would be perfect in the role. When Paramount flew Siddig over they told him it would just be for the weekend; soon after his arrival he was told that they wanted him to relocate permanently. Siddig had to fly back to London, move out of his apartment and fly back to Hollywood immediately.

Siddig is single and eager to explore America during the time between the seasons of the series. He has little time for sightseeing during the production week which often con-

sists of ten to sixteen hour days, particularly when an episode prominently features his character such as "Rivals" did. He has a place in West Hollywood and is making a life for himself away from the studio in a place very different from his native England.

Working on DEEP SPACE NINE has been an interesting experience for the young actor, particularly since some fans have found the brash Dr. Bashir to be a bit on the abrasive side. Siddig has found that at some STAR TREK conventions, fans have transferred their annoyance with Julian to the actor himself. While he has been taken a bit taken aback by these fans Siddig does agree with their appraisal of the character. However, in the second season of the series Dr. Bashir has become a far more dimensional character and one who is less brash and more self-aware.

## Romance is where you find it

Discussing his experience working on this American TV series, Siddig told STARLOG that STAR TREK is not exactly a minor show in Great Britain, either. "It's quite popular back home in England. Everyone knows STAR TREK, the original series, and everyone has heard of THE NEXT GENERATION. Fewer people have seen it, but it's getting more popular every day." American TV shows do not premiere in Europe immediately; European audiences sometimes wait six months to a year before they see a new American show. In England, TV stars are not treated quite the same way as they are in the United States. "In England when you're known, you don't become hounded or get sent letters by people you don't even know."

His character is still expresses arrogance but now he has a direction and a purpose, as when he encountered the title character in the episode "Melora," who was even more arrogant than he. Dr. Bashir seemed much younger in the first season of the series than he does now. The character is more self-assured and is no longer mooning around after the unapproachable Dax. Bashir and O'Brien have been paired off in at least three episodes so far, beginning with "The Storyteller," and have become something of an odd couple. Bashir is the fussy, proper sort while O'Brien is more gritty but lacking in patience as well.

Offstage Siddig has struck up a real-life romance with actress Daphne Ashbrook, who played Melora, Julian's love interest, in the DS9 episode titled "Melora." That's Hollywood!

# CHARACTER PROFILE

# LT. JADZIA DAX

Jadzia Dax is a Trill, a joined being comprised of two entities that exist in a symbiotic relationship. Her external humanoid form is that of Jadzia, a beautiful young woman of twenty-eight, possessed of great intelligence and charm. The symbiont, Dax, is a sluglike being that is every bit as intelligent as its host, and has lived for over three hundred years. Dax was once part of Toban Dax, a specialist in pre-warp engines, primarily dealing with sub-impulse thruster configurations. Dax said that Toban knew coil inverters like no one else, even if he had no imagination (and barely any sex life).

Jadzia is Dax's seventh host. Having become joined with Dax, Jadzia now shares all his knowledge, memories and wisdom, including all recollections of its twenty-year friendship with Commander Benjamin Sisko while living in its previous host, Curzon. But this is a symbiotic relationship; the symbiont's personality always merges and interacts with that of the host to some degree. Each succeeding host/symbiont pairing is as much a new person as it is a continuation of the symbiont's ongoing existence. It is a complex life: Dax has fathered two children, and given birth to three. Curzon Dax was in many ways a mentor, as well as friend, to the young Benjamin Sisko. To this day, Sisko sometimes addresses Jadzia Dax privately as "old man" despite the recent switch in gender.

The history of the Trill is, as might easily be imagined, a fairly intriguing one. Many hundreds of years ago, the invertebrate, androgynous and sluglike symbionts lived sep-

Terry Farrell in uniform at 1992 Deep Space Nine press conference. **Photo c 1994 Alvert L. Ortega**

arately from the humanoids. The symbionts dwelt in a subterranean realm, and the humanoids lived on the surface of their planet. A major environmental disaster made it crucial that the two species learn to work together. This relationship eventually evolved into a symbiotic one; the slugs were unable to live on the surface without a host. Not every humanoid Trill becomes a host, however, and most of them live their lives as single entities. This indicates that the humanoids outnumber the symbionts to a considerable degree. Once joined, a Trill is one entity: one coherent personality is synthesized from two distinct components. The symbiont merges with the host.

When Curzon died, Dax was implanted in Jadzia's body through a surgical procedure placing it in her abdominal cavity. In fact, Jadzia had the ambition to be a Trill host since she was a child. Being a Trill host is a highly complicated and competitive procedure, and Jadzia was one of the top candidates of her generation. She underwent long and arduous training and testing— mental, psychological and physical— to discern if she was qualified to serve as a host. She excelled at all. In the academic world, she was unparalleled. Long before she was joined with Dax, she earned doctoral degrees in a wide variety of scientific fields, including zoology, astrophysics, exoarchaeology and exobiology. Combined with the generations of scientific knowledge contained in the mind of the symbiont Dax, the joined Jadzia Dax is an expert in an astounding array of fields—technical, cultural and scientific.

## The Secret in Space

Jadzia Dax first arrived at Deep Space Nine shortly after her commanding officer, Commander Benjamin Sisko, took charge. One of her shipmates on the voyage out was the new doctor who volunteered to work on the station, Julian Bashir. In the course of their voyage he began an ongoing flirtation with this attractive young woman, unfazed by the presence of a three hundred year old slug inside her body.

After renewing Dax's friendship with Sisko, the Trill examined the mysterious Orb that Sisko had brought back from the surface of Bajor. The alien artifact triggered in her a startlingly vivid reliving of the transfer of Dax from the dying body of Curzon to her own flesh.

Soon, Jadzia Dax joined Sisko on a dangerous mission to the Denorios Belt, an area near Bajor where the mysterious orbs, as well as Odo, were found. There they witnessed to the opening of a wormhole and, despite their attempts to escape, are soon drawn into its vortex. Once they got through to the other side, Dax discovered that they were in the Gamma Quadrant, seventy thousand light years away from their previous location. Dax thus became one of the first two Federation "discoverers" of this region, although it would probably be more accurate to say that the wormhole discovered them. Back in the wormhole, they stepped out and found themselves together in a strange alien landscape, each perceiving it differently.

An orb enveloped Dax and carried her back to the station, leaving Sisko behind. Ever the scientist, Dax was back to work immediately, despite the remarkable experience she just had. She played a crucial role in forestalling the inquisitive Cardassians while helping Chief Miles O'Brien achieve the impossible feat of relocating the space station to a vantage point near the mouth of the strategically vital wormhole. In her first outing on Deep Space Nine, Jadzia Dax proved herself to be a truly amazing being.

## Past Master

An interesting question, and one that involves the very nature of a joined Trill, came to the forefront in the episode fittingly entitled "Dax." In this outing, Jadzia Dax was almost kidnapped by alien intruders. The reason for this abduction attempt opened a whole new can of worms, so to speak. It seems that thirty years before, Curzon Dax was involved in the civil war on the planet Klaestron as a Federation diplomat. General Ardelon Tandro, a key player in the war, was killed and became a martyr around whose memory the winning side rallied. When Sisko captured Dax's escaping abductors, one of them proved to be Tandro's son, Ilon. Evidence had come to light that implicated Curzon Dax as the murderer of the famed general, and Ilon has come to take Dax to trial. The abduction seemed necessary because DS9 is under Bajoran legal jurisdiction. The Bajorans have no automatic extradition arrangements with the Klaestrons, longtime allies of the Cardassians.

A hearing was held to determine if Dax can be removed— and if, in fact, Jadzia Dax can be held accountable for the actions of Curzon Dax. But Jadzia herself remained curiously silent on the matter of the charges against Dax. This puzzled Sisko, but he could pry no information from his old friend. Odo went to Klaestron to investigate the background of the case, and discoverd that Curzon Dax had been a friend of the dead General—and more importantly, of the general's widow, Enina. She herself refuted the notion that Dax killed her husband, and felt that her son was unduly obsessed with his dead father. Only after this discussion did she discover that Curzon Dax is gone, and that the symbiont Dax has now merged with Jadzia.

The most perplexing thing about this case is the behavior of Jadzia Dax herself: she has nothing, literally nothing, to say about the accusations against her. It is up to Sisko to defend the character of Curzon Dax, while Ilon must struggle to prove that Jadzia Dax and Curzon Dax are one and the same. These are fascinating philosophical questions about the nature of the Trill, but the real drama here comes to light when Odo finally puts together a

Terry Farrell.

highly reasonable hypothesis that Curzon Dax and Enina Tando had an affair. Dax reluctantly admits that this is true, but will not speak about it publicly; there is a great deal of honor among the Trill, and Dax will not do anything to damage the reputation of the woman Curzon Dax loved.

The debate raged, and Ilon seemed on the verge of possible victory, when his own mother arrives, interrupts the proceedings, and provides Curzon Dax's alibi for the time of the murder: he was with her. Curzon Dax had sworn to keep this secret, both to protect the reputation of Enina and the reputation of General Tandro. It would not do for the people of Klaestron to know the truth that their great hero, General Tandro, had died while trying to betray his own side! The question of responsibility among the Trill still remains a difficult one, for Jadzia Dax's silence was a result of her intent to keep the promise made by Dax's previous host, Curzon.

## Master of the Game

All in all, Jadzia Dax is an intriguing character. While she has many interests, perhaps her real hobby is foiling the amorous intentions of Dr. Julian Bashir. Dr. Julian Bashir was quite obsessed with winning her. Although she may be attracted to him, she is primarily amused by the situation. After all, she's been a man several times herself, which takes some of the mystery out of sex for her. She is particularly amused when, in "If Wishes Were Horse," Julian Bashir's ideal version of her—crazy about him, somewhat vacant, and utterly submissive—somehow becomes an actual entity. This other Jadzia Dax proves to be quite annoying after a while, so the real Jadzia Dax, like the embarrassed Bashir, is quite relieved when she disappears. This experience helped Julian to understand that the Dax he imagined was quite different from the Dax in reality, and his amorous attentions have since gone elsewhere.

Once, Julian approached Jadzia while the Trill was engaged in a meditative state as she played an Altonian Brain-Teaser. The doctor was unable to keep the bubble-like sphere supported with a perfect calm, which would have resulted in complete control of the neural Theta waves that produce the sphere. When the sphere loses its integrity following the transfer from Dax to Bashir, Jadzia comforts the doctor, telling Julian she had been trying to master the game for 140 years. Julian noted that Dax had cold hands, which she admitted was a peculiarity of the Trill, to which Julian responded, "Cold hands, warm heart."

The depth of their relationship can best be described by the fact that Julian trusted Jadzia with his personal diaries. When Julian and Miles were believed killed, Dax confessed that she had yet to read the journals. Kira suggested that Jadzia keep them.

## Dax and Miles

Jadzia Dax and Miles O'Brien respect each other as Starfleet officers even though O'Brien is still getting used to the fact that Dax has hundreds of years of experience and a body that has distracted more than a few young ensigns. He has learned to enjoy Dax's sense of humor yet fails to understand why she would spend time playing cards with Quark and his Ferengi companions. Dax would patiently explain the reasons, but it made no sense to O'Brien. O'Brien would stop by Quark's for a drink but he would not trust a Ferengi as far as he could throw one (albeit he could probably throw a Ferengi a considerable distance). He thought Dax could make better use of his free time.

O'Brien is is drawn to Dax's competence and calmness during a crisis. When an assassination plot against Vedek Bariel failed, it was Dax who helped O'Brien out-think the computer lockouts to discover that the weapons detection grid had been knocked out, allowing the assassin, backed by Vedek Winn, access to the Promenade with her weapon.

## The Other Alien

Dax and Odo have perhaps more in common than any of the other denizens of Deep Space Nine. Each is different from the other humanoids with whom they work. Odo, as a shapeshifter, has physical abilities far beyond the range of his crewmates; Dax, with the wisdom and memories of several lifetimes, which gives her perspective that the other crewmates cannot achieve. She finds solutions that might stymie the logic of a shorter-lived person. Dax and Odo have never been romantically linked but the two do have a special comradeship that transcends their individual species.

Perhaps the most harrowing event of Jadzia's life occurred in "Invasive Procedures," when a disgruntled Trill who'd been turned down for "Joining" hijacked the station with the help of some Klingon mercenaries. The Trill forced Bashir to transplant the symbiont Dax from her body into his own. But the unbalanced Trill could not cope with the change, and Sisko eventually managed to stun him. Dax was returned to Jadzia by Bashir, who struggled heroically to keep her alive long enough for the return of the symbiont.

Jadzia Dax is a fascinating character. As a beautiful young woman with the accumulated knowledge and wisdom of three hundred years, Jadzia Dax will certainly go far in her career. When her life ends, many years from now, the symbiont Dax will find a new host who will always remember the life of Jadzia.

Terry Farrell.

Photo c 1994 Alvert L. Ortega

# ACTOR PROFILE
# TERRY FARRELL

Born in Cedar Rapids, Iowa, Terry Farrell became a professional model at age 17 when she signed up with the Elite modeling agency in New York City. She spent three years working as a model and cover girl for such magazines as MADEMOISELLE and VOGUE.

She moved to Los Angeles in 1984 and made her TV debut with Daryl Hannah. Both played models in the short-lived 1984 ABC series PAPER DOLLS; Terry's character was Laurie Caswell, an intelligent model. One of her other co-stars on the show was Jonathan Frakes, who would enter the STAR TREK universe ahead of her in 1987 on STAR TREK—THE NEXT GENERATION.

Terry made guest-appearances on FAMILY TIES and THE COSBY SHOW. Other TV work included a role in the movie BEVERLY HILLS MADAME with Faye Dunaway. In the TV movie DELIBERATE STRANGER, about serial killer Ted Bundy, she played one of the victims of star Mark Harmon. Terry also appeared in an episode of the new TWILIGHT ZONE in the remake of the classic TZ story "After Hours," in which she played a mannequin who came to life at night. Terry had another fantasy role, guest-starring in one of the best episodes of QUANTUM LEAP, "Leap For Lisa." She played a nurse whom the Dean Stockwell character is accused of murdering in the 1950's.

Terry has appeared in a variety of films, including the Rodney Dangerfield comedy BACK TO SCHOOL. She played the reporter Joey Summerskill in the horror movie

HELLRAISER III: HELL ON EARTH which was released in the summer of 1992. It was this film where she would be seen and subsequently called to test for DEEP SPACE NINE.

On the day she auditioned for Deep Space Nine, Terry had two other auditions. She didn't expect to land the DS9 part because she knew that the series had been casting roles months before she ever walked through the door. After she completed her first reading for Deep Space Nine, they wanted her to read another scene. She had to make her next audition so, that same day, she drove up to Universal in Studio City and then back down to Paramount in Hollywood to read for Rick Berman and director Dave Carson. Two days later, Paramount was negotiating a contract with her agent, however, she still had not been given the role. She had to audition twice more during the following week before the producers were certain.

## The Nature of the Trill

Jadzia Dax, the Trill, was a character who was refined from a type of alien introduced on an episode of STAR TREK—THE NEXT GENERATION called "The Host." Originally Dax was to have been the character later named Melora who was featured in the second season episode of the same name. Melora was a character from a low gravity world which required her to use a high tech wheelchair in the gravity of Deep Space Nine. Although they ultimately decided to go in a completely different direction with Dax, the episode "Melora" demonstrated just how interesting this character could be. She could "swim" in zero gravity and reveled in such this environment which she could activate in her private quarters.

Terry Farrell was the final actor cast among the regular cast of DEEP SPACE NINE. In fact, filming on "The Emissary" had already begun and director Dave Carson scheduling scenes around the uncast role of Dax. Farrell was reportedly one of the only actresses testing for the part who was able to grasp the concept of the character. Jadzia Dax, of course, is a Trill named Jadzia with a symbiont named Dax living in side of her. Jadzia Dax is the latest form of Dax who has lived in many bodies, the previous one having been that of a man. Now a female, Dax, although a merged personality with Jadzia, is able to look at life through new eyes and react to the different way the entity is treated by people. Some of the actresses testing for the part actually thought they would have to try to talk in a deep voice, like a man.

### Dax Makes the Deadline

Originally the Trill in "The Host" had a different look requiring heavier makeup. Two days into the shooting of "The Emissary," it was decided that this was not the look they wanted. Michael Westmore designed the simplified look for the

Terry Farrell.

Photo c 1994 Alvert L. Ortega

Trill. Terry had to film two days' worth of scenes over again with the new Trill look, consisting of the interesting circular pattern up one side of her face. In "The Host" the Trill was unable to use the transporter, a facet of the character which has been altered for the new improved Trill seen on DEEP SPACE NINE. By the time the makeup question had been resolved, all of Dax's scenes had to be filmed in one week, resulting in some 16 hour days.

As played by Terry Farrell, Dax has emerged as truly one of the more interesting characters on the series. The fact that Dax is not only able to ignore Quark's sexist remarks, so much so that she actually enjoys the company of the Ferengi. She explained to Kira in one episode why she finds the Ferengi fascinating in spite of their many negative personality traits, confessing that over the several hundred years of life Dax has come to find the Ferengi the most interesting people they have ever met.

Terry Farrell plays Dax as both a young woman and a person possessed of a great deal of knowledge and experience. She exudes confidence as Dax has had many generations to make mistakes and to learn from these mistakes. This aspect of Terry's character is periodically examined, such as in the early first season episode titled "Dax" which explored in detail the true nature of a Trill. The current host is obligated to take responsibility for the past deeds and misdeeds of the symbiont inside them.

Terry says that that being part of the ensemble cast of Deep Space Nine is like working in a theatre company of actors. "It's a special feeling to feel that safe at work. We're so lucky because there aren't any ego problems. Everybody is very professional. This is very different from other things I've worked on. I wasn't prepared for this. I think the fact we all get along gives and have this chemistry really makes the show work, as it has for the other two STAR TREK casts."

# CHARACTER PROFILE

**ODO**

Security chief, alien, shapeshifter: Odo's origins are shrouded in mystery. Fifty years before the arrival of the Federation at Deep Space Nine, he was discovered adrift in a spaceship in the Denorios asteroid belt near Bajor. The newfound being had no memory of who he was or where he originated. Named Odo by the Bajorans who discovered him, he lived on Bajor for many years after his discovery. Able to transform himself into any object—a chair, a pencil—he was regarded as a freak by many, which may account for his grim and isolated personality. He opted to take a generally humanoid form in order to function among the races, Bajoran and Cardassian.

Odo is actually not a humanoid at all, but a shapeless blob. He must daily return to this amorphous state or risk serious damage to his health. Therefore he spends part of each day in a bucket. He resents being obliged to take a humanoid form, but this resentment only emerges in his humorless cynicism and his frequent exasperated observations about the absurd behavior of the humanoids. The Cardassians ruled Bajor and Deep Space Nine with an iron fist and they were the authority figures with which Odo dealt. Although not overly fond of their ways, nor always approving of their methods, he appreciated the Cardassian inclination to pursue order.

Rene Auberjonois in uniform at 1992 Deep Space Nine press conference.

**Photo c 1994 Alvert L. Ortega**

## Lawman

In time Odo became the head of security on the station. The head Cardassian, Gul Dukat, trusted Odo because of his sincere interest in justice and the fact that he was immune to all temptations. Money, food, sex and the vices of most humanoids held no interest for the shapeshifter, who may not actually even possess a natural gender; no one knows for sure. Gul Dukat was willing to risk the occasional instance where Odo's impartiality would conflict with Cardassian political interests. This was preferable to giving the job to an ambitious Cardassian who might use the position to build a power base, and this was a great deal easier than co-opting a Bajoran for the job. A Bajoran in the position of security would very likely have been a member of the Bajoran resistance, something Dukat could not risk.

Then, of course, there is Quark. Never an out-and-out felon, he was nevertheless the person most likely to be involved in any criminal activity on the Deep Space Nine station. This fact, combined with the knowledge that the Ferengi philosophy invariably conflicts with the laws of other cultures, made Quark a prime focus of Odo's watchful eye. Quark is probably Odo's main adversary. Paradoxically, if anyone could be described as Odo's friend, it would be Quark. Friend or enemy, Quark is the one person with whom Odo has an actual working relationship. Ever pragmatic in his search for justice, Odo sometimes trades on small infractions to gain Quark's unwilling aid in larger matters. Quark usually thinks he's getting the better of Odo but their goals are so radically different that Odo often comes out at an advantage. All in all, the relationship between Odo and Quark is a real give and take, which both aliens seem to relish.

## The More Things Change...

It was quite a remarkable tribute to Odo's honesty that the Federation—and the Bajorans—allowed him to retain his position as security chief on the Deep Space Nine station. This role appealed to him. When the Cardassians left, they stripped both planet and space station of everything of value. In the ensuing chaos, Odo clearly saw himself as a much-needed preserver of law and order, as well as a force for continuity. Much to Odo's chagrin, Commander Sisko also felt that Quark was an equally important force for continuity, and asked the Ferengi to stay as well. So their cat-and-mouse game can continue indefinitely.

Odo prefers working with Commander Sisko and the Federation to working with the Cardassians. But he sometimes misses the fact that his job was, on a procedural level at least, a great deal simpler during the Cardassian occupation. Sisko first encountered

Odo shortly after his arrival on the station. Called to apprehend some thieves, Odo soon almost has them at bay when one throws a deadly weapon at him. Here Odo reveals his amazing shapeshifting powers to Sisko, bending the middle of his body out of the way of the weapon. When the criminal remains belligerent, Sisko fires a phaser blast into the air to end the conflict. Odo astounds him by telling the new Commander that no weapons are allowed on the Promenade, and promptly confiscates Sisko's weapon! Odo doesn't bend his beloved rules for anybody, not even his own superior officer. The other thief is Nog, Quark's nephew, probably put up to the theft by his own family members.

Odo was at first perplexed by Sisko's desire that Quark remain on board the space station, but soon understood the reason. Odo cannot help but admire Sisko's ruthless use of Nog's situation to force Quark to his way of thinking. Later, when the Cardassians renew their interest in the station and in Bajor after the wormhole appears, Quark demonstrated without a doubt that his loyalty is to the security of the station. Disguised as the bag in which some "lucky" Cardassians place their winnings after "winning" big at Quark's casino, Quark boards their ship and disables their sensor array and other systems. He thereby enables Sisko and Dax to leave the station in a runabout without being detected.

## Odo and Kira

Odo is always pragmatic, and is dryly bemused by procedural matters. When Lursa and B'Etor, the Klingon sisters of the late Duras, show up suspiciously on Deep Space Nine (in the episode "Past Prologue"), Odo thinks the best way to forestall any trouble is to alert the Klingon government to the presence of these renegades and then hand them over. He is hardly surprised, though, when Commander Sisko prefers to watch and wait. (Sometimes, if Odo had his way, there wouldn't be much happening in any given episode of the show!) Dryly, he comments that life under the Cardassians was easier. Is there a glimmer of cynical humor in Odo's acerbic comments? Perhaps. But Sisko's does approach gives viewers the chance to see a rat observing a shady Klingon transaction then morphing into Odo. He's the perfect undercover cop!

This episode also examined the relationship between Odo and Major Kira Nerys. It seems they have known each other for a long time. In fact, a later episode ("Necessary Evil") would reveal that they first met during the Cardassian occupation. Back then— which was also about the time Quark opened up for business on Deep Space Nine— Kira was a prime suspect in a murder investigation. Odo never solved the case, largely due to an alibi provided to Kira by the avaricious Quark. Some day, another case would reveal that Kira had actually been on the sta-

Rene Auberjonois.

Photo © 1994 Alvert L. Ortega

tion as an operative of the Bajoran underground, and that she had killed the victim, although it was in self-defense. Though this discovery would come later, Odo's near-friendship with Kira has always held a lingering doubt from the case. This doubt surfaces in their discussion regarding Kira's mixed feelings about the presence of another Bajoran undergrounder on the station, one who is regarded as a terrorist even by other Bajoran freedom fighters. His efforts to enlist her in a mission actually proves, by episode's end, to be highly destructive. Odo demonstrates his sense of justice by instructing Kira that she needs to examine where her loyalties lie, and which course of action would be best for Bajor.

Of course, in his tenure as security chief on Deep Space Nine, Odo has had plenty of dealings with freedom fighters and/or terrorist. In "A Man Alone," , Odo warned a middle-aged Bajoran on the Promenade that he has twenty-four hours to leave the station. Sisko later questioned Odo's action and Odo explained that the Bajoran, Ibodan by name, is a dubious character from the Bajoran underground. Although regarded as a hero by many due to his opposition of the Cardassians and their rules, he was, in Odo's eyes, nothing more than an opportunistic black marketeer.

## Old Debts

According to the shapeshifter, Ibodan once let a girl die because she could not afford his price for a black market drug. Later, Odo managed to convict the man for murdering a Cardassian, but when the Cardassians left, the provisional government of Bajor set the "hero" free. Sisko was adamant that Ibodan's presence is not technically illegal, but Odo is determined to get the man off the station. He sums up his philosophy by saying: "Laws change depending on who's making them, but justice is justice." Odo's commitment is to justice, on a very deep level, not to trivial and transitory rules. But to outside ears, this sounds dangerously like a man ready to go to any lengths to settle a personal grudge.

When Ibodan is murdered in a holosuite, a classic variation of the locked-door mystery scenario, suspicion falls on Odo, and Sisko must remove the shapeshifter from the investigation. To make matters worse, the Bajorans on the station are soon stirred up against Odo, goaded by a bearded Bajoran no one has seen before. We soon see how isolated Odo is from the other beings he must deal with in his lonely life. Luckily, there are those who share his sense of justice, and who stood beside him against mob violence. Dr. Bashir managed to uncover the bizarre truth: Ibodan cloned himself, murdered his own clone, and left the holosuite, explaining why DNA traces only revealed the presence of Ibodan. The bearded man is actually Ibodan in disguise. Ibodan is unpleasantly surprised

when Odo arrests him for murder again— this time for killing his own clone!

This storyline revealed the real odds with which Odo deals every day. Unaware of his own origin, forced to live among and mimic the shape of aliens, he is truly a being alone in the universe, with only his own moral code to protect him. He was further isolated in the episode entitled "Babel." He was one of the few characters not afflicted by the aphasia virus left on the station by terrorists. When the crisis peaks, Odo has no choice but to accept Quark as an ally.

Odo's resourcefulness and courage are undeniable. These traits are exemplified by his willingness to go face-to-face with the hunting aliens who invade Deep Space Nine in "Captive Pursuit." Like Sisko, Odo is appalled by the nature of the hunt involving Tosk,. He is not too territorial to protest loudly when O'Brien insists on escorting Tosk to alien custody; and he is sensible enough to pick up Sisko's hint when O'Brien helps Tosk escape. He is,

# DEEP SPACE NINE CREW BOOK

after all, more interested in justice than he is in mere protocol.

## Odo Investigates

Odo is particularly challenged by the near abduction of Jadzia Dax by Klaestron intruders. The Klaestron insist that Jadzia be charged with a murder they say was committed by Curzon Dax, years earlier. Odo is bent out of shape (figuratively speaking, not literally) when these intruders almost manage to sweep Dax off the station right under his nose. Playing detective, Odo begins to suspect that the widow of the murdered man is holding back something. Examining communication records, he develops the hypothesis that Curzon Dax and this woman were having an affair at the time of the murder— not necessarily good news, as far as Sisko is concerned, since all that Odo has managed to turn up is a reasonable motive for murder! However, once Odo confronts the woman with this theory, she comes

to the trial and provides Curzon Dax with a perfect alibi: he was sleeping with her at the time of the murder. Here, Odo looked beyond the obvious and brought justice to bear once again and, in the process, saved one of his compatriots on Deep Space Nine.

Odo takes his position on Deep Space Nine seriously, perhaps too seriously. He is loath to surrender any of his authority. Even so, in "The Passenger," he allowed—with his usual lack of humor—a Starfleet security officer named Lieutenant George Primmin to take charge of security measures surrounding a crucial deuridium shipment to the station. As Primmin takes charge, one of the most compelling mysteries of Odo's career was unfolding. Rao Vantaka, a murderer who has left a trail of death across the galaxy in the past twenty or thirty years, arrived on the station. Vantaka was a prisoner of Ty Kajada and arrived only to die in Doctor Bashir's arms. Vantaka will going to make trouble anyway: it seems that Ty Kajada, after having tracked her prey for twenty years, is not convinced that he is dead, as he has convincingly faked his own death many times in the past.

Vantaka was on his way to steal the very deuridium shipment that is about to arrive. Deuridium is particularly valuable to Kobliads, the species to which Kajada and Vantaka belong, because it can actually be utilized to extend their life spans. The apparently deceased Vantaka was particularly obsessed with life extension—at least with the extension of his own life, since he seemed to place little value on the lives of others. Odo had to cooperate with Kajada in her efforts to make sure that the criminal is really dead.

The shapeshifter really had his hands full with Vantaka, Kajada, and Primmin. Odo soon found that all his files— and all active files on the station— have been wiped from the computers. Odo's annoyance at Primmin's presence led him to offer his resig-

nation to Sisko, who assured Odo that he is still in charge of all security on DS9.

## Behind the Scenes

Not surprisingly, Odo's nemesis Quark was involved in Vantaka's scheme. The wily Ferengi assumed that the deal was off when Vantaka died, but was surprised to see a shadowy figure with Vantaka's voice insisting that the deal is still on. Dax, meanwhile, had studied Vantaka's effects and found that he had been working on a viable means of transferring consciousness from one body to another. Dax and the Doctor agreed that Vantaka's pursuer Kajada was the most likely suspect in this scenario. Odo was thus obliged to exclude Kajada from any further involvement in the investigation. However, it is really Dr. Bashir who has been taken over by Vantaka. The resolution of this episode really tests Odo and the crew of Deep Space Nine. In the end, Meanwhile,

Odo finds Lieutenant Primmin to be a real asset in the investigation. He reconsiders his original harsh judgment of the young officer, who appears again on at least one more episode of Deep Space Nine. So we see that, despite his harsh ways, Odo can be. . . flexible.

In "Vortex," an alien named Croden is involved in a robbery planned by Quark, but kills a Miradorn in the process. In custody, Croden is in danger of being killed by the Miradorn's surviving twin. Odo must prevent vigilante justice from claiming his prisoner's life. Croden has something that might interest Odo: he claims to have visited a planet in the Gamma Quadrant where there are shapeshifters, an entire civilization of them. He shows Odo an artifact containing a mineral which transforms, right before Odo's eyes, into metal, and then back again. He tries to win the shapeshifting constable's sympathies with the alluring possibility of an answer to the riddle of Odo's origins. He claims to

know the way to the shapeshifter colony on an asteroid in the Chamra Vortex.

They discover that Croden is wanted on several charges on his home world of Rakhar. He is considered to be an "enemy of the people." Commander Sisko assigns Odo to take the prisoner Rakhar and hand him over for extradition. The voyage is complicated by the pursuit of the Miradorn, who will, if he must, kill Odo along with Croden in his quest to avenge the murder of his twin. The Miradorn attacks just as the runabout arrives near the Chamra Vortex. Because the Miradorn ship completely outclasses Odo's runabout, Odo decides to go into the Vortex, where ionized gases hide them.

## A Hint of the Future

Finally, they land on the asteroid on which Croden claims to have encountered the shapeshifters. Odo soon realizes that it was a ruse: Croden's daughter is in a hidden cave, in a stasis device. His daughter is the only survivor of Croden's family; the repressive government of his world killed his wives as punishment for his political opposition. When the Miradorn attacks, they move the girl to the runabout. They elude the Miradorn who, firing on the asteroid, is destroyed when the gasses surrounding his ship explode. Convinced that Croden is a man driven to desperate measures by the cruel injustice of his home world, Odo reports that the man was killed on the asteroid. He then finds Croden and his daughter passage on a Vulcan ship. As a token of gratitude, they give him the shapeshifting pendant—perhaps it will someday serve as a clue to his background.

Once again, we see that Odo's primary motivation is justice. When he realizes that Croden is the victim of institutionalized injustice, he is more than willing to lie outright in order to help the man and his daughter find a better, more peaceful future.

Odo's vulnerable side came to the fore in "The Forsaken," when he is trapped in a turbolift with Lwaxana Troi! In this episode, Odo captures a thief who stole Lwaxana's prized jewelry. The notorious Betazoid woman becomes fascinated with Odo and starts giving him more attention than he would like. A series of systems failures assail the space station and the two are trapped together. Here we learn a lot about Odo: raised in a lab on Bajor, he was used as a source of amusement. He was asked to change into any object the researchers imagine, animate or inanimate.

Odo's confessions are soon interrupted as the end of his daily cycle grows near, and he must revert to his liquid state. No one has ever seen him in that state before (except, presumably, the researchers who "raised" him) and he is somewhat embarrassed by its approach. To put him at ease, Lwaxana Troi removes her bright red wig, revealing the more ordinary real hair beneath. Then she forms her skirt into a pouch into which

Odo flows. This scene is an interesting encounter in lowered defenses.

Later, Lwaxana Troi hints to Odo that their next encounter might be intimate in another manner entirely. Needless to say, Odo has never met anyone quite like her, but it seems he finds her style intriguing. Of course, humanoids are generally interesting through the eyes of an amorphous shapeshifter.

## Justice is Justice

In the relatively short period of time that has elapsed since the end of the Cardassian occupation, Odo has decided that the Federation, and its local representative Commander Benjamin Sisko, are infinitely preferable to his previous experiences as an employee of the fascistic and militaristic Cardassians. And so he stays. Perhaps the Gamma Quadrant on the other side of the newly discovered stable wormhole near Bajor will reveal Odo's origins, but he has yet to pursue that possibility as it would mean abandoning his hard-earned position on the station. Although he does not know much about his species, he is certain that justice is an integral part of their culture. Odo does not always follow the letter of the law: he believes that laws change but justice forever remains the same.

# ACTOR PROFILE

# RENE AUBERJONOIS

Rene Auberjonois was born in 1940 in New York City. Rene came from an artistic family: his father was a writer and his grandfather a well known Swiss painter. His father was a news correspondent so not only did they live in New York City and Rockland County but also lived in Paris and London

Because of Rene's background, he was naturally interested in pursuing a career in the arts. Although today he known for his roles on television and film, he started on the stage. Rene began his stage work when he was 16 under the tutelage of his family friend and mentor, actor John Houseman. "My parents wanted to see if I was really serious about becoming an actor, so I became an apprentice at a theater in Stratford, Connecticut. They asked John to see if I had any talent, feeling that I was at an age to be easily influenced—away from the business—if I had no talent. But John told them, 'Your son is an actor.' " He would later teach mask work at the Juilliard Drama School, again under the guidance of John Houseman. Other family friends included Burgess Meredith and Alan Jay Lerner.

Rene completed high school in London. He returned to America to attend college at Carnegie-Mellon University in Pennsylvania. He graduated with a Bachelor of Arts degree in Drama. Upon graduation, Rene moved to Washington, D.C. where he began acting professionally on the Arena Stage and traveling to cities such as Los Angeles and New York. Rene also lived in other cities. In San Francisco he co-founded the American

Rene Auberjonois.

Photo c 1994 Alvert L. Ortega

Conservatory Theater. In New York he helped found the Brooklyn Academy of Music Repertory Company and in Los Angeles he was instrumental in the formation of Mark Taper Forum.

## From Stage to Screen

To actors, the Broadway stage is a pinnacle of achievement. Rene made his Broadway debut in the musical "Coco" with Katharine Hepburn. For this role he won the Tony Award; he also received a Tony for his performances in the Broadway stagings of "Big River" and "The Good Doctor." But one of the best known Broadway roles for which he won a Tony was as the character Buddie Fidler, the movie mogul, in the musical "City of Angels." Other stage work included appearing with James Earl Jones in the late1970's Joseph Papp production of "King Lear." He also has had roles in "Richard III" and "Metamorphosis."

Rene Auberjonois made his film debut in

1970 for director Robert Altman in the hugely popular movie M*A*S*H. He appeared in Altman's next film, Brewster McCloud. This was quickly followed by McCabe and Mrs. Miller, Images, Pete 'n Tillie, and the 1976 TV movie Panache. Other films he has appeared in include The Hindenberg (with George C. Scott); the 1976 version of King Kong; The Eyes of Laura Mars, and Police Academy 5. His latest film is The Ballad of Little Jo.

Rene also does his share of voice acting. He was the voice of the cleaver-wielding chef in the modern Disney classic The Little Mermaid. He also was the voice of a character in the 1992 release of Little Nemo in Slumberland and he was the voice of Peter Parker/Spider-Man on a Spider-Man phonograph record released in the late 1970s.

## Radio and Television

Rene also has produced and directed plays for National Public Radio. In Europe he appeared in and narrated the mini-series Ashendon for BBC television. Rene has won the Emmy Award twice: for the ABC presentation of The Legend of Sleepy Hollow and for Best Supporting Actor in a Comedy for his role of Clayton Endicott III in Benson, on which he co-starred for six seasons. He has made guest-appearances on such TV shows as Matlock, L. A. Law and Civil Wars. On Showtimes' Faerie Tale Theater, he appeared in "The Frog Prince" and "Sleeping Beauty." He also appeared in More Wild Wild West and Wild Wild West Revisited, 1970's reunion movies of the old TV series.

Prior to being cast on Deep Space Nine, Rene appeared in Star Trek VI— The Undiscovered Country as Colonel West, one of the conspirators. He did only one day's worth of work on the film as a favor for his old friend Nicholas Meyer; at the time was never even told the name of his character. Much of his part was cut from the theatrical release but later restored when the film released on video. Rene did not realize that his scenes had been restored until he was informed by some fans at a Star Trek convention. His appearance in this film brought him to the attention of the producers of Deep Space Nine and led to his testing and eventually being cast in the pivotal role of Odo, the shape-shifting security chief.

## Home on the Range

"When I read the pilot script of Deep Space Nine I saw this wonderful character; I was very excited. I see a lot of scripts and this was something special. I met with the Star Trek people and it was no easy task. They put me through a lot of hoops to get the part. I went back four or five times to convince them I was the actor—they were looking for actors for all the parts in London, New York, and everywhere! They were really on quite a search. It was huge. I have a lot of friends who went up for the role of Odo and other parts. It was a real coup to get the role and I'm just loving it!"

Nana Visitor told Superstar Facts magazine, "Rene is one of the most fun people I've ever met. He's got the best stories; he's a very vibrant, happy soul and we've gone out to dinner, the whole families. We've gone to his house for dinner—he's an incredible cook, as is his wife. In the back of Bon Appetit they always ask celebrities, 'If you could choose three people to have a dinner party with, who would they be?' Rene Auberjonois would be one of mine because he's that much fun."

Rene and his wife, Judith, are indeed gourmets; they cook based on experience and never write their receipes. Rene's hobbies also include painting and photography. He maintains a studio in his home where he can work on his avocations. He shot photographs in Honduras while working on a film and had an exhibition when he returned. Recently he has been photographing the extras on the sets because he finds them more natural.

## A Pop Culture Icon

Ordinarily Rene does not like to watch his own work. However, during Deep Space Nine, Rene has consistently studied his performance. "I've always been a little uncomfortable watching myself. It's hearing your own voice on a tape recorder: it makes you uncomfortable. When you work on stage, you give the performance and it goes out into the void. There's a finite number of people who see it and then it's gone forever. I just accept that as part of what I do."

He believes that his background in theater is perfect for his role on Deep Space Nine. "It was a natural for me. If you're going to do pop culture, Star Trek is the closest thing to classical theater. There's nothing else like it." But what he didn't expect after all his years in show business is the sudden increase in notoriety he's experienced. "I've been doing this for 30 years. I am not an overnight discovery. I also didn't take this job thinking that I was about to

Rene Auberjonois.

become part of pop culture; it is such a phenomenon. I am just beginning to get an inkling of what this is all about. I didn't consider this when I took the job. It just came along at a really good time. I have two kids in college and I wanted to do steady work. I didn't think about becoming a pop culture icon."

The sound stage where Deep Space Nine is filmed is next to one used by The Next Generation, which made for an interesting introduction to the cast of TNG late one night. "One night we were working deep into the night. We were all growing tired when, all of a sudden, the door burst open to the set and Patrick Stewart, Jonathan Frakes and Brent Spiner danced in singing, 'Good morning! Good morning!' They were working late that night, too, and it was their way of welcoming us and saying, 'You see what you're in for!?' "

# CHARACTER PROFILE

QUARK

Quark is a Ferengi so he is, by definition, a sly fox, ready to sell out his best friend for gold. But the proprietor of the gambling establishment on the Promenade at Deep Space Nine is a surprisingly complex person. At times he is an irredeemable sexist pig, drooling over Dax and flirting shamelessly with Kira. He is capable of heroism if pressed and, all too often, of villainy.

Quark had run the establishment on the space station for five years under the Cardassian occupation and made a great profits in the black market. He was preparing to leave the station, due to the instability of the provisional government on Bajor, when the Federation stepped in to help the planet. In an attempt to cash in one last time, Quark sent his nephew Nog and a B'kaazi named Jas-qal to clean out the ore samples in Section A-14. Nog was apprehended in the act and Sisko used a form of Ferengi plea bargain so Quark could remain on the station. By making Quark a community leader, Sisko was able to convince other merchants to stay at the decrepit station. Quark was the bait.

Quark likes Bajorans, yet he complains that they make a dreadful ale. The Ferengi insists he never trusts ale from a God-fearing people or a Starfleet officer who has a member of his family in custody. Quark likes Bajorans because they leave him alone, with the exception of the enormous amount of red tape with which he must deal.

Quark preferred working for the Cardassians. They were brutal and deceitful and

Armin Shimmerman as Quark at 1992 Deep Space Nine press conference. **Photo c 1994 Alvert L. Ortega**

Quark had taken advantage of their vices, making profits from Cardassians seeking escape from the harrowing duties of an occupying army. Quark also served the Bajorans who sought their escape in the seclusion of a holosuite. Widows and orphans in the refugee camps would use their imagination to forget the harsh realities of their existence. Quark was always ready to make a dream come true— as long as he got the gold-pressed latinum.

## The Skilled Opportunist

Quark is a wheeler and a dealer. He might be small potatoes compared to the some of the hotshots and big ears in the Grand Nagus' entourage, but he has everything a Ferengi needs to make a killing in the cutthroat world of galactic commerce: an eye for opportunity, a talent for behind-the-scenes intrigue, and plenty of that ultimate Ferengi virtue— greed.

Quark does not appreciate the implication that

he is simply a bartender. His establishment on the Promenade is more than a bar or a gambling den—it is the place to be in that sector of the galaxy, especially after the discovery of the wormhole, a magnet for business opportunities both legitimate and illicit.

On Deep Space Nine's bustling Promenade, Quark is the unproclaimed king of commerce. He has a hand in everyone's business to some degree, if not in their pockets as well. He hears about everything on the station; and so his nemesis, Constable Odo, is often forced to turn to Quark for information no one else can obtain.

Quark's business interests are varied, encompassing all forms of entertainment.. The bar is the center of operations— it is here that he meets the varied aliens, humans or otherwise, who pass through the station and provide him with grist for his greedy mill. The gambling houses— specializing in Dabo and other games of chance and often rigged by Quark— are a real generator of the gold-press lat-

inum. Upstairs, the holo-suites caters to any fantasy. Quark certainly keeps up-to-date on the latest developments in erotic holo programs—a Ferengi is as sensuous a being as he is avaricious, especially in the highly erogenous ear zone.

## Grace Under Fire

Quark is well-versed in Ferengi politics. Odo once observed that Quark had all the character traits of a politician. When Zek, the Grand Nagus of all Ferengi, decided to retire, he named Quark to take control of the Ferengi Alliance. Zek was actually using Quark to get his son to show some initiative. The son joined forces with Quark's brother, Rom, and attempted to assassinate Quark. When Odo saved Quark, the Ferengi demonstrated what humans would consider an unusual response: instead of being furious with Rom, he embraced his brother for his ambition. Rom probably wished he had tried to kill Quark sooner. Quark enjoyed his brief time as Grand Nagus, even if Odo did refuse to kiss his scepter.

The station and several key crew members have been saved by Quark on occasion. On the other hand he has helped invaders take over the station and even hired assassins and aided them in obtaining a runabout. His best moments came when he took command at Ops during an aphasia attack that sidelined every being except Quark and Odo. This was perhaps Odo worst nightmare: marooned on Deep Space Nine, quarantined with Quark. Kira was stunned to hear Quark welcome her back to the station when she returned with a scientist who was able to find a cure for the airborne disease.

Another high point for Quark occurred when the Ferengi agreed to Odo's offer to become his deputy (as opposed to becoming his prisoner). Quark discovered the secret location of the "Circle's" headquarters. The Bajorian revolutionary army, led by Minister Jaro Esso with support from fundamen-

talist Vedek Winn, was planning to torture and kill Major Kira. With Quark's crucial information, Sisko and Bashir were able to free Kira. Quark's intervention also saved Bajor from the Cardassians, who were secretly funding the attempt to overthrow the weakened provisional government.

Quark's low points include hiring mercenaries to take over a cargo ship. He led them to the runabout, but was surprised to find that Dr. Bashir was the assassin with which he was doing business. In fact, Bashir was being dominated by an alien body thief.

## Breaking the Rules

In a more serious infraction, Quark allowed a group of mercenaries—led by a renegade Trill—to bypass security and enter the station. Deep Space Nine had been running with a skeleton crew due to a massive plasma storm, so Quark allowed the complex to be captured. This misadventure nearly turned tragic when the

Trill stole Dax, the symbiont, from the body of Jadzia, the host. The newly created Dax was about to leave the station, which would have led to Jadzia's death, when Sisko risked the symbiont's life and shot the renegade host with a phaser. The host was stunned and Dax was returned Jadzia. Quark hated the fact that he caused Jadzia pain and so he led the escape attempt and enabled the crew to regain control of the station.

Quark does like Dax, for Ferengi live for fantasies and possibilities. She is kind to him and often meets with him for card games—quite remarkable since females are normally forbidden. Dax gets an honorary exemption, as a Starfleet officer and former man. Kira cannot understand why Dax spends time with "Ferengi vermin," but Dax enjoys the manner in which Quark and the other Ferengi enjoy life. She gets annoyed with their behavior on occasion, but she, in the case of the renegade Trill, she understood that Quark did not want to injure her. He thought the thieves would simply buy some stolen gems and leave; he was unaware of their real intentions.

Quark had a recent romance that can only be described as bizarre. An ambitious new Ferengi had become a favorite of Quark's due to "his" ideas and knowledge of all the Rules of Acquisition, and their proper applications. Quark is overcome with odd confusion when his assistant, Pel, suddenly kisses him while on a business trip to the Gamma Quadrant. Even more embarrassing, others witnessed the kiss. Quark is relieved to discover that his assistant is a female but his relief is temporary: he passes out when he realizes he has broken every Ferengi law in the book by doing business with a female. He is saved only by the fact that the Grand Nagus, himself, was doing business with her. To use the law against Quark would also invoke it against the Nagus.

## Paying the Consequences

Quark admired the woman's fortitude, yet was so caught up in Ferengi beliefs that he had trouble picturing women as being clothed and taking part in business. Ferengi women are kept nude, pregnant and ignorant on purpose: otherwise they would beat the socks off Ferengi men. But Quark has learned to interact with females of all species. The sexy Boslic freighter captain, for example, provided him with the key earring which led to Kira and Miles' trip to Cardassia IV to rescue a Bajoran hero. He even managed to negotiate with the unpleasant Klingon sisters, Lursa and B'Etor.

The wily Ferengi has tried to be open-minded. Quark and Kira have developed unusual friendship that overcomes their mutual animosity. The key to understanding Quark is examine the love/hate relationship he has with his mortal enemy, his antithesis, the bane of his existence, and his best friend— Odo. Quark, Kira and Odo form a complex trio whose interaction on the Cardassian ore processing station sets the stage for their time together on Deep Space Nine.

Now that Starfleet has command and the Bajorans administrate, Quark will perform an occasional good deed, but only the result is a reasonable profit. He does not have the same moral code as the others. For example, he sees nothing wrong with theft. For Quark the only problem with theft is the possibility of getting caught. Yet the Ferengi does have a code of conduct. He was outraged when a former colleague robbed and killed a man during a business deal that he had arranged. Quark is far from the typical Ferengi, but even farther from the typical Starfleet officer. Sisko allows him to stay in business, refusing to enforce Starfleet regulations as long as Quark's games are (relatively) honest and fall within Bajoran rules and regulations. It is unclear what Sisko really thinks of Quark. While Sisko seems to find him amusing, he has also made it obvious to the Ferengi that he can close down his business at any time. Thus Quark remains wary of crossing Sisko's path.

## The Odo Connection

Quark was the first regular to locate on the Promenade of Deep Space Nine. He had met Kira Nerys the night before he met Odo when Kira paid him to supply her with an alibi. Odo was appointed by The Prefect of Bajor, Gul Dukat, to investigate the murder of a Bajoran who collaborated with the Cardassians. Odo visited Quark to check out Kira's alibi. At first Quark supported Kira's story, but when Odo threatened to charge Quark as an accomplice to the murder, he admitted she had paid for the alibi. Odo does not like Quark yet the two do begin to build a relationship—one that neither will address. When Odo was suspected of murder, Quark was one of the few to come to the shapeshifter's defense. He

Armin Shimmerman

Photo c 1994 Alvert L. Ortega

told the Bajoran bigots that Odo was neither a killer nor a collaborator. When reminded that Odo was his worst enemy, Quark noted Odo came the closest to being his friend.

Because of their five year history together on Deep Space Nine, Odo knows perfectly well of what Quark is capable, and thus knows exactly when to consider him a suspect in something nefarious. Odo will not hesitate to confront Quark and accuse him outright of a specific crime; he usually has more than enough proof to implicate the Ferengi. Quark sometimes has to do some fast talking and even faster sidestepping to direct Odo to someone even more guilty than Quark—which is not to say that the Ferengi was completely innocent of the specific crime, simply a little bit guilty.

Odo and Quark have something of a truce. The security officer frequently stops by to needle Quark, particularly when he discovers that Quark has been the victim of someone else's shenanigans. Odo has

actually saved Quark's life. In "The Nagus," the Ferengi was targeted for assassination. Without the timely intervention of the security chief, Quark would have been blasted out of an airlock. Odo will allow Quark a long time to repay this debt.

The two have a playful sparring arrangement, with Quark often demanding payment for his help. Quark constantly reminds Odo of his duties. Odo makes it clear to the Ferengi that he will not mourn Quark's passing; he even suggests that he will happily partake in the Ferengi tradition of purchasing and selling a piece of the corpse, for even in death a Ferengi can make a profit.

## Rom the Devious

Quark can inevitably be found behind the bar. Although his brother Rom works for him in the bar, Quark does really trust him—he is a Ferengi, after all. Rom has demonstrated cleverness at times but, more often, he displays deviousness. However Rom is not very bright, insuring that he will forever be under his brother's thumb. Quark and Rom are brothers but are far from being equal partners in running the gambling establishment on the Promenade. Rom has tried to kill Quark: attempting first with explosives, joining forces with the son of the Grand Nagus; and then sending him out an airlock without a pressure suit. Interestingly, Quark was proud of Rom for showing initiative by attempting to kill him and take over the bar.

Quark recently had to reevaluate Rom's intelligence. He had always assumed that Rom was an idiot but his brother showed that he could work an electronic lock pick and use chemicals to burn into Quark's safe. Rom showed remarkable skill, yet dubious judgment, in letting Quark know he could get into the storeroom as well as Quark's floor vault. Odo is not so naive, telling Rom, "You're not as stupid as you look," to which Rom replies, "I am so!"

## Major Kira Nerys

Kira has little love for the being she refers to as a "little troll," but the two have worked together, when forced. Kira endures Quark's incessant flirting and cannot understand how Dax can be friends with the Ferengi. Quark did earn points with Kira when he brought her the earring of Li Nalas, as that allowed her and O'Brien to track down the Bajoran freedom fighter on Cardassia IV. A beautiful Boslic freighter captain gave the earring to Quark, who in turn gave it to Kira. Quark was actually responsible for saving Kira's life when he discovered the secret hiding place of "The Circle," where Kira was being tortured for Starfleet information.

When Vedek Bareil visited her quarters on the station, she admitted that Quark was a friend. However, Kira was outraged when Quark's when his failed attempt to fence stolen jewels led to a renegade Trill and his Klingon accomplices taking control of Deep Space Nine. Since

Quark is a Ferengi he is an incurable sexist and revels making advances towards Major Kira. When she violently rebuffs him he merely becomes more excited with the possibilities should she succumb. When he once put his hand on her waist and she threw him against the wall he happily stated, "I love a woman in uniform!"—a particularly interesting comment since Ferengi women traditionally wear no clothes.

## Dax, O'Brien and Bashir

Quark is infatuated with Jadzia Dax, the lovely Trill whom he often serves Roctageno and spice pudding. Quark feels he was victimized when his attempt to fence stolen jewels led to Dax being removed from Jadzia; he had no idea the mercenaries would attempt to steal the symbiont from the Trill. He started the rescue attempt, faking injury to get to sickbay, then helping Bashir free Odo.

Quark provides a sympathetic ear to Miles O'Brien. Miles is amused at some of Quark's antics, yet he finds that Quark does listen. Quark encouraged O'Brien to risk his life and violate the Prime Directive to help Tosk, when the alien prey was pursued by hunters from his homeworld. Quark is on O'Brien's repair list, but Miles would just as soon give the Ferengi a wide berth.

Quark finds the libidinous of Doctor Bashir amusing, yet fails to interact with Julian in most situations. Dr. Bashir treated Quark after members of the "Circle" branded their logo on Quark's head. Later, Quark was nearly killed when he was shot in the chest with a Compressed Tetryon beam set to kill: Quark had found a list of Bajoran collaborators for the widow of the man whose murder first brought Odo to Deep Space Nine. Julian was able to stabilize Quark. Quark survived the injuries and a subsequent assassination attempt in sickbay and eventually identified his attacker.

## A Question of Stature

The Ferengi did not exist until Star Trek—The Next Generation. The Klingons were now friends of the federation and in "The Last Outpost," the Ferengi were to replace the Klingons as the new antagonists. However, somewhere between conception and execution the Ferengi were not created to be imposing characters: unlike the tall, powerful Klingons, the Ferengi were five feet tall. Prior to "The Last Outpost," which introduced the Ferengi, a reference was made to the Ferengi being so fearsome that even the Klingons felt threatened by them. Once introduced, however, the Ferengi were hard to take seriously. At first they wielded powerful electric whips but the whips were never seen after "The Last Outpost." By their second appearance a few episodes later, in "The Battle," the Ferengi were portrayed as the ultimate businessmen.

## Rules of Acquisition

The word "greed" would best define the Ferengi race. Although it is well known that they will do anything for a profit, the Ferengi consistently deny reports that they are unscrupulous, branding them as vicious rumors. Yet, without fail, members of the Ferengi race demonstrate a willingness to achieve success with underhanded methods. The Ferengi operate under a code called the 285 Rules of Acquisition. For example, rule 21 is "Never place friendship above profit"; rule 33 is "It never hurts to suck up to the boss"; and rule 48, "The bigger the smile, the sharper the knife."

At times the Ferengi seem to possess one mass personality—an obnoxious one. They live and breathe predatory capitalism and practice it in every underhanded manner possible. Receiving stolen goods is not considered a bad thing—unless you get caught, and no one can whine and weasel like a Ferengi. They consider the

Armin Shimmerman

cedes them: being distrusted makes it more difficult to pull a fast one in a business deal. Getting the better of someone in a deal is a must for the Ferengi. They tend to deal with other races because dealing with each other becomes a nasty duel.

Unlike Sisko and some of the others, Quark is no newcomer to Deep Space Nine. When it was controlled by the Cardassians, Quark was there, running his operations and bribing officials to look the other way when his games were investigated for being fixed. The Cardassians appreciated the entertainment services offered by Quark's Place, particularly the range of sexual programming in the holosuites. To Quark nothing is too kinky so long as there is a profit in it for him. The Cardassians are masters of exploitation, themselves, so they respect the Ferengi; however that does not mean they trust them. Rather they knew exactly what to expect from Quark. Quark was ruthless in business and the Cardassians were ruthless in everything.

law and order represented by the Federation to be something of a nuisance and dislike the "do-gooder" mentality that the representatives of the Federation impose. The Ferengi also dislike the fact that their reputation pre-

## The Deal Maker

Quark has been known to exhibit a range of emotions, from greed to cowardice. When a former business partner was sent to a Romulan prison camp for a deal with Quark that went sour, the Ferengi showed both fear and cunning as he attempted to bribe his way off the man's death list. Fate played into Quark's hands as the criminal chose to commit more crimes rather than accept Quark's generous bribes; these crimes led to the thief's undoing.

Commander Sisko tends to have as little to do with Quark as possible. Sisko did prevent Quark from closing his place and fleeing the station after the Cardassians left; Sisko knew that he could not convince all the merchants to remain on the station, but if Quark stayed then many of the others would stay as well. There must be money to be made anywhere Quark operates: the Ferengi calculates his profits not weekly, but hourly.

Quark justified his decision to remain behind on Deep Space Nine by stating that the Federation would bring new business to the station. The Ferengi could not have anticipated, however, that the only stable wormhole in the galaxy would be discovered nearby, making the space station a key stopover point for commerce with the otherwise distant Gamma Quadrant. Previously Bajor was a remote outpost and now it was one a major hub of the entire galaxy. New visitors would be arriving at the station daily. Suddenly Quark's reluctant decision to remain on became the best business decision in his life.

## Insider Trading

Quark deals in information as though it were a commodity and he uses it to remain in Sisko's good graces. Although Commander Sisko does not trust Quark, he and the entire senior staff know what to expect from the Ferengi. While they do not imagine that Quark will develop a taste for honesty overnight, Odo insures that Quark is regularly made aware of the penalties associated with a serious violation. When Quark is caught cheating he is forced to make restitution, which is particularly painful for a Ferengi. After all, giving back hard earned latinum is like giving up a piece of his own flesh. This form of punishment is opposed to a Ferengi's basic instincts, but Quark is willing to accept it—perhaps as a challenge. After all, the key word is caught. Getting around the rules is one of the first skills a Ferengi learns; other people's rules are merely obstacles to overcome.

"Quark's Place" contains the primary entertainment concessions on the space station. When visitors stop at Deep Space Nine on their way to the Gamma Quadrant or upon arriving in the Alpha Quadrant through the wormhole, they invariably visit Quark's establishment. They can find gambling of all kinds as well as holosuites. Originally the holosuites were only brothels but under pressure from Commander Sisko these have been reprogrammed for family entertainment such as baseball and other non-sexual interests.

## Always an Angle

But what is Quark like beneath that ruthless veneer? He has been shown to be capable of any number of things, both good and bad. In "The Passenger" he helped supply mercenaries to a serial killer who planned to hijack a shipment which would be passing through the space station. When Vantaka's hijacking failed, Quark managed to elude prosecution as an accessory in the crime. The fact that Quark would willingly deal with a murderer showed a disturbing side to his "anything for a profit" motivation.

Quark is more than willing to let someone else do the time for his crimes. When he and a cousin sold defective warp engines to some aliens, Quark implicated his cousin who went to prison instead of Quark. Similarly, he engineered the hijacking of some Romulan ale on which he was the middleman. When the Romulans caught the thief, Quark eluded involvement and his henchman did eight years in a Romulan prison camp. Another cousin stole some rare items from a museum and was caught trying to sneak aboard the space station, presumably to meet with Quark. Although the Ferengi denied involvement, Quark was clearly crestfallen to hear about his cousin's capture.

On the other hand, when Quark discovered that his new partner, Pel, was actually a female Ferengi in disguise he relinquished all interest in a deal with the Nagus—a deal which would have been worth millions—in order to protect her and grant her free passage to the Gamma Quadrant. Clearly Quark felt something for Pel and did not want to see her hurt. We saw a compassionate side to the Ferengi, a side never before seen. Clearly, Ferengi are not just one-dimensional cartoons capable of expressing only negative personality characteristics.

## A Charming Ferengi?

Quark is, despite his studied exaggeration of socially agreeable behavior, actually a fairly charming representative of his species—although he is prone to overdo it from time to time. "My benevolence is known throughout the galaxy," he crows at one point, and one can only wonder exactly how little truth lies behind that grandiose statement. Perhaps this strangely repulsive charm is what makes Commander Benjamin Sisko so oddly tolerant of Quark; or perhaps Sisko realizes that the vigilant Odo makes it unnecessary for Sisko to worry much about Quark's shady doings.

Occasionally Quark even helps solve a problem, as long as there's something in it for him. For example, he agreed to a shutdown of the casino to fool some Cardassians in

"The Emissary." Sometimes all that's in it for Quark is simply the continued benevolence of the authorities. Sisko has his power and knows how to use it; and Quark knows how to get along with those in power. After all, he opened his business up under the ruthless Cardassian occupation.

## Bravery Within Limits

When it comes to physical confrontation, Quark is essentiallly a coward, although he proved otherwise at least once by attacking a Klingon in "Invasive Procedures." Quark pretended to be injured and was taken to Sickbay so he could team up with Doctor Bashir . Together they overcame, by trickery of course, one of the desperadoes who had taken over the largely abandoned station. Attacking a Klingon— even ineptly— takes quite a bit of courage. Quark may have been moved to this act because he was the one who gave the criminals access to the station, not realizing that their goal was to steal the symbiont Dax from Jadzia's body. Quark certainly had no desire to see Jadzia die. Not only is there no profit in her death, but he truly likes her, perhaps because the Trill seems to like him. Quark makes amends and saves the day, using his sensitive ears and highly developed Ferengi lock-picking skills to free Odo from a containment box. He does pause a moment before letting his nemesis out of the box. There may be a conscience between those huge lobes somewhere after all. In "Move Along Home," he is caught cheating at Dabo by visiting Wadi, the first aliens to officially come across from the Gamma Quadrant. He is forced to play their game known as Chula. Slowly, Quark suspects that the four game pieces he is moving in this game— whose rules he does not even know—represent Commander Sisko, Doctor Bashir, Major Kira and Dax. Their lives hinge on the outcome of the game and so Quark adjusts his playing accordingly in order to optimize their survival. In fact, they were never in real danger, but Quark never knew that and he actually swears that he will never cheat again. Only time will tell about this particular Ferengi oath— wagers, anyone?

## Business as Usual

Sometimes Quark lives dangerously. He sets up criminal activities, mostly thefts and robberies— although his vast information network, which even Odo cannot help but admire, probably involves theft of information as well. But when a robbery planned by Quark results in the death of a twinned Miradorn raider, Quark and Rom scramble to keep this information under wraps, since the surviving Miradorn is bent on revenge and will certainly kill them both— especially Quark— if he learns of their involvement. Luckily, the Miradorn is killed pursuing Odo and the man who pulled the trigger, leaving the Ferengi brothers in the clear. Their only regret is that the vengeful Miradorn did not somehow dispose of Odo before his untimely demise. This is a victory of sorts for Quark— although he could not get his hands on the valuable artifact he desired, at least he didn't get caught.

And so it's business as usual for Quark— because for a Ferengi, life is business. Watching the universe from the comfortable hub of his thriving establishment, Quark is located in the ideal spot to sense new opportunities for profit. His head spins with dreams of more gold-press latinum for his coffers— but with both feet on the ground, he pursues his single-minded goal with great practicality, distracted only by his ongoing feud with the dour Odo. It would be hard to imagine Deep Space Nine without him.

Armin Shimmerman

Photo c 1994 Alvert L. Ortega

# ACTOR PROFILE
# ARMIN SHIMMERMAN

Armin Shimmerman is an interesting and amusing performer who brings a lot to his characterization of the Ferengi. Underneath a great deal of makeup, the actor is able to use his eyes and his voice to bring a depth of feeling to Quark. Armin was born and in Lakewood, New Jersey and moved to Los Angeles when he was seventeen. Originally Armin wanted to be a lawyer, which some might argue is perfect career training for being a Ferengi. He got involved in acting when his mother urged him to join a local community theater as a way of making friends and meeting new people. He had roles in high school productions and then college productions at the University of Southern California (USC).

After graduation from USC, Shimmerman moved to New York City to pursue stage acting. Armin appeared in regional productions of the Tyron Guthrie Theater, the New York Shakespeare Festival and the American Shakespeare Festival. On Broadway he had roles in the productions of "St. Joan," "Three Penny Opera" and "I Remember Mama." He also played Jacques in Shakespeare's "As You Like It." Armin is particularly interested in the works of William Shakespeare and has written and directed a theatrical seminar called "Shakespeare In A Nutshell."

## Television Beckons

He returned to Los Angeles where he started getting regular work on a variety of TV shows, including Who's the Boss, Alien Nation ( in the episode "Gimme, Gimme"), L.A. Law, Married with Children, and Cop Rock. His first real recognition on a television series came when he played Pascal on Beauty and the Beast. He worked on this series for two and a half years. As Pascal he had to wear makeup, and while this might seem like good preparation for what was to come, it was nothing compared to what he would experience on Star Trek—The Next Generation and Deep Space Nine. Prior to joining Deep Space Nine, Shimmerman had a semi-regular role as Cousin Bernie on the critically acclaimed but low-rated series Brooklyn Bridge.

Shimmerman actually worked on Star Trek before Quark was ever conceived. He was the voice of the talking wedding box in the first season Next Generation episode titled "Haven." He played the villainous Letek, one of the first Ferengi, in "The Last Outpost." He also appeared as Bractor, yet another Ferengi, in the TNG episode "Peak Performance."

## Transported

Working on "The Last Outpost" was an interesting experience for Armin. He had not seen any of the sets before reporting for work, and because of his three hour make-up routine he had to arrive on the Paramount lot extremely early. After completing his makeup, while it was still dark outside, he went to the "planet stage," a huge sound stage on which the elaborate sets representing the surfaces of other planets are constructed. Shimmerman recalled, "I had to go through a door that was in complete darkness. I opened a second door and I walked onto another world! I think everyone who watches Star Trek has a similar experience, although in a different way; they are transported to another world. In my case, I was literally transported to another world!"

Armin regrets that the director played up the comedic aspect of the short, funny looking characters so much so that at the end of the episode the Ferengi were hopping around like monkeys. "If you look at the pilot for The Next Generation, they make the Ferengi sound as though they might be the new Klingons. The director of that episode looked at these three very short character actors in all this rubber and he thought they were funny. And they are comical! But I think he changed the threat into parody. That's certainly not what I brought to my original audition. The Ferengi have become more and more comical, although they're not monkey-like any more."

## Making Up the Time

While some actors dread sitting in a makeup chair for hours on end

while they are transformed into some otherworldly character, Armin Shimmerman takes it in stride. He goes out of his way to mention how much he likes it, because of all the overtime he makes. Three hours are required to apply the Ferengi makeup early in the morning and another fifty minutes are required to remove it. The costume worn by the typical Ferengi was designed by Next Generation costumer Robert Blackman.

Michael Westmore developed the Ferengi makeup so that the actor would still be able to make facial expressions rather than simply wear a mask as in the old Planet of the Apes. Westmore's Emmy Awards for makeup prove that his approach is superior. Quark's features are built up in pieces. After the head piece goes on, makeup is used to blend around the actor's eyes; the ear pieces are added, which are the most prominent characteristic of the Ferengi; and a touch of scarlet is added around the eyes.

The most distinctive feature of the Ferengi face

are the teeth, made from an alginate which the actor slips on over his own teeth and held in place with Poligrip or Fixodent. Armin is very happy with the teeth because they do not interfere with his ability to speak.

## Acting Under Rubber

Karen Westerfield, Michael Westmore's assistant, applies the makeup. Karen won an Emmy for her work as part of the Next Generation makeup team in 1992. Armin uses the time it takes for the makeup to be applied to gradually get into character; when he is halfway through the three-hour process he has transformed himself mentally into the wily proprietor of Quark's place.

Nana Visitor, who plays Major Kira, a character who despises Quark, says about Armin, "A lot of my enjoyment of that relationship is because of Armin Shimerman. He's an incredible actor! To act that well covered in rubber is just really impressive. I love any scene I have with him."

Not long after Deep Space Nine went on the air, Shimmerman started making appearances at conventions. He is not expected to make a speech—the fans just want to see the actor in person. To Armin it is little more than a news conference, just as his November 1993 appearance at Universal Studios was an informal question an answer period. He was clearly in his element fielding questions with the other cast members, playing off what they had to say and interacting humorously with them. While Quark may not officially be close friends with the senior officers, Armin Shimmerman is clearly close friends with the entire cast.

Regarding the advantages of playing a role under such elaborate make-up, Shimmerman states, "It gives me the freedom to do the most outrageous things, things that I don't think I could do bare-faced."

# CHARACTER PROFILE

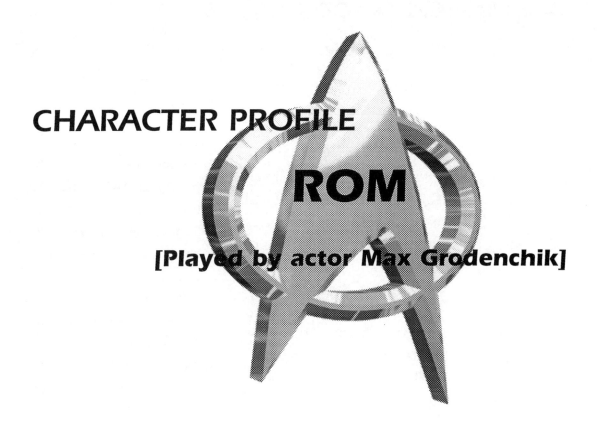

# ROM

## [Played by actor Max Grodenchik]

Bumbling, inept, doltish and altogether useless—these are probably some of the kinder words that the Ferengi Quark might use to describe his own brother, Rom. Quark is usually exasperated with his sibling; Rom cannot complete any task to Quark's satisfaction. He has the essential greed that makes a Ferengi a Ferengi, but he obviously lacks the basic skills to carry any schemes to a successful end, much less fulfill the simplest functions as Quark's subordinate. Quark really makes a mistake when he explains the sudden recovery of his rundown replicators as the result of Rom's repairs. It is no wonder Odo investigates and learns that Quark is sneaking off and using the replicators in empty crew quarters. Nobody would believe for a minute that Rom could fix anything— only that he could break it easily.

Quark tolerates his brother, it would seem, because the Ferengi value their families; or perhaps this tolerance is some sentimental peculiarity of Quark's. Quark definitely suave compared to Rom and Rom secretly resents his brother's knack for success. He will take the opportunity to plot against Quark, but only when Quark is at an extreme disadvantage. Nog lacks the courage to take chances. When the Grand Nagus apparently dies after appointing Quark as the new Nagus, the gullible and jealous Rom is easily drawn into the plans of the Nagus' son Krax, who feels that the title should have been his.

### Rom to the Rescue

Perhaps Rom was a poor choice for a co-conspirator, since all of their attempts to assassinate Quark fail miserably. Even so, once the real Grand Nagus returns and lets Quark get his life back to normal, and Rom's role in the assassination attempts is revealed, Quark is so impressed that he promotes his brother to assistant manager of Quark's. "I didn't think you had the lobes," he tells Rom. Unfortunately, this may have inspired Rom to further attempts to oust his brother, in the misguided belief that he will be more successful without Quark. In fact, Rom would probably be lost without his smarter brother, so it is just as well that he is too incompetent to get rid of Quark. For the most part, he serves merely as Quark's underling, where Quark can keep an eye on him.

Rom's only glimmers of intelligence were revealed when he confessed to Quark that he knew ways of opening locked doors ("Necessary Evil") and suspected that something wasn't right about the Ferengi named Pel ("Rules of Acquisition"). Rom's attempts on Quark's life were balanced out when he saved his brother's life. An assassin attacked Quark in sickbay and Rom's helpless screams brought security on the double ("Necessary Evil"). Only after Rom realized that he had saved his brother from the assassin that he started screaming all over again: he had blown his one big chance to fill Quark's shoes!

# CHARACTER PROFILE

## NOG

### [Played by actor Aron Eisenberg]

Nog, the son of Quark's brother Rom, is probably the most unusual Ferengi we've seen yet in the Star Trek universe. He is certainly the youngest. He and Jake Sisko have a great deal in common. Both are being raised on a space station in a distant corner of the galaxy, far away from their home worlds. Neither has a mother, which in Nog's case is probably due to the Ferengi custom of keeping their women sequestered and apart from the male-dominated society. Both of them like girls. Although an odd pairing, Jake and Nog became friends. Nog played a crucial role in keeping Quark on the space station. Ben Sisko used him as a pawn to keep Quark, and commerce, in place on Deep Space Nine. And although he's a mischievous child who gets Jake Sisko into trouble, he is a faithful friend as well.

Their friendship comes under strain in "The Storyteller," when the Tetrarch of a Bajoran faction called the Paqu arrives to negotiate an ancient boundary dispute on the station. The holder of this hereditary title is a pretty fifteen-year-old Bajoran girl named Varis. Both Nog and Jake are smitten immediately. This position is very difficult for a young woman of her age and she is prone to tantrums and obstinacy. She does even have parents to turn to for advice, due to the murderous Cardassians.

Nog, determined to meet her, is surprised to find her in the very spot where he and

Jake like to sit and observe the goings-on in the Promenade. Nog wonders aloud whether the group that disputes her border might not have something of use to her side. In due course, Nog and Jake counsel her away from the negotiations! The Ninth Rule of Acquisition seems to make sense to her when Nog quotes it verbatim. Nog manages to get into mischief, even here, and convinces his friends to stand watch while he breaks into Odo's office to steal the Constable's bucket. The heist complete, he stumbles and pours a bucketful of a viscous liquid over Jake. Fortunately, the liquid is only oatmeal; unfortunately, Odo appears and is not amused. At least Varis has diplomatic immunity. Eventually, she finds a solution to her negotiations, inspired, it seems, by Nog's second-hand tidbits of Ferengi philosophy. She awards the happily astonished Nog with a kiss on the cheek.

## An Educated Ferengi?

It is a little uncertain if Nog is getting an ordinary Ferengi upbringing on Deep Space Nine. Attending classes at Keiko O'Brien's school is certainly not the usual course of a Ferengi's education. Even after Rom bans Nog from going to these classes, Jake Sisko secretly tutors him, so this young Ferengi is learning a few things the average Ferengi does not know.

Still, he is a Ferengi through and through, as demonstrated in the episode "Progress." Perhaps inspired by his success with Varis, he decides to strike out into business and enlists the aid of Jake Sisko. One of Quark's underlings foolishly ordered a large quantity of yahmok sauce, which only Cardassians can tolerate. Quark is incensed, but Nog feels his lobes tingle—a sure sign of impending opportunity. He knows that he can get a bar or two of gold-press latinum out of this somehow.

After Nog gets Quark's permission to get rid of the

stuff, Nog and Jake manage to trade the sauce for an even larger quantity—100 gross—of self-sealing stem bolts. The two young entrepreneurs do not even know what these bolts are and neither does the one man who should know, Chief O'Brien. Resourcefully, Nog tracks down the name of the man who originally ordered the stem bolts but declined to accept the order because it cost too much. Wisely, he reasons that the man might be more inclined to buy them at a discounted rate. The Bajoran barters over the radio, and agrees to swap some land to the pair, who now call themselves the Noh-Jay Consortium. Nog agrees, but is convinced that he has made yet another useless trade.

He is elated, some time later, to overhear a very interesting conversation between Odo and Quark. The Bajoran government plans to build a recycling plant on the land owned by the mysterious Noh-Jay consortium, which seems to be based on Deep Space Nine. With more than a bit of a swagger, Nog walks over to his uncle with a business proposition which will cost the older Ferengi five bars of gold-press latinum. The quest for profits may actually be ingrained in the Ferengi psyche after all, and young Nog is no exception. It remains to be seen how he will turn out, influenced by Jake and a human education; in any case, Nog will certainly become an unusual representative of the Ferengi race.

# CHARACTER PROFILE

# ZEK, THE GRAND NAGUS

## [Played by actor Wallace Shawn]

The ultimate leader of the Ferengi—and by extension, the greediest, most avaricious Ferengi of them all—the Grand Nagus is an ancient Ferengi indeed, his immense earlobes lined with countless wrinkles and wispy white whiskers. An incredibly feeble-seeming and blustery old being, he clearly has a vast intelligence and is dedicated to pursuing to the fullest extent the Ferengi ideals of accumulation. When he comes to host a Ferengi conference on Deep Space Nine, it becomes obvious that if this is the top Ferengi, then Quark holds a position somewhere near the bottom.

The Nagus enjoys the best things in life despite his advanced age and starts off his visit to Deep Space Nine with an extended stay in one of the more morally questionable holosuite programs. The Grand Nagus Zek has at least one son, an ambitious Ferengi (as if there were any other kind) named Krax. The conference is an incredible convocation of the greedy, as top Ferengi from all over the galaxy converge on the bar known as "Quark's Place" to discuss the exploitation possibilities of the Gamma Quadrant—a place where the reputation of the Ferengi does not precede them.

Quark feels like a lowly bartender until the Grand Nagus, himself, compliments him on his foresight in opening his business near the wormhole. This should give a clue to how conniving the Grand Nagus really is—after all, Quark had been there for years, and there was no way he could have foreseen the discovery of the Wormhole. At the conference, The Grand Nagus rallies the Ferengi with the prospects waiting on the other side of the wormhole, only to announce that he is too old to continue to guide them. "Not as greedy as I used to be," he tells them, an astonishing admission which stuns them all.

The members of the conference are more stunned, though, by his next words: the replacement as Grand Nagus will not be his son Krax, but the bartender Quark! They are not only surprised, they are incredibly angry, and storm out of the conference. Overwhelmed by this new responsibility, Quark asks the Nagus Zek for advice, only to have the ancient Ferengi greed-meister drop dead right in the middle of their conversation. Left to his own devices, Quark will soon discover that the fringe benefits of being Nagus are marginal when compared to the hazards, such as frequent assassination attempts.

Of course, this is all part of an interesting and elaborate plot by Zek, who is really very much alive. Krax manages to auction off preserved parts of his father's body (an honored Ferengi tradition) while the Nagus, who had entered a deathlike sleep trance, returns intact.

## The Way to the Gamma Quadrant

Back in action, Zek reveals that the entire plot was a test to see if his son Krax deserved to become Grand Nagus. The Nagus' son failed the test. Krax, aided by Quark's brother Rom, was behind the many attempts to assassinate Quark. According to the Nagus, this direct, forceful approach shows that Krax isn't very good at greed: it is better to be subtle, and gain power behind the scenes. If Krax had some-how co-opted Quark, keeping him as the nomi-nal Nagus while pulling the strings from a discreet van-tage point, the Grand Nagus Zek would have been impressed. However, he must now re-assume the mantle of greed and power that he has worn for so long, until he can locate a suitable replacement. This episode provides proof that there is subtlety even in the Ferengi way of life, and that such subtlety, however rare, is to be valued in the highest reaches of power and accumulation.

The Grand Nagus returned when negotiations to deal with the Gamma Quadrant were becoming more intense. He used Quark and his new associate, Pel, to assist him. Quark manages to make an important contact in the Gamma Quadrant with someone who will lead them to "The Dominion"; without their approval, no one can do business in the Gamma Quadrant. This information would have proved profitable for Quark had not Pel turned out to be a Ferengi female. Shocked, Zek agrees not to report Quark for doing business with a female, primarily because Zek was tricked as well. Zek does, however, withdraw his offer of sharing the Gamma Quadrant profits with Quark because Quark insists that Pel be allowed to go free. Zek does not see the profit for Quark. Since Zek benefits in both the short run and the long run, Pel's fate does not matter to him.

Thus, the ancient Nagus revels in his position of power, although he can't quite understand why Major Kira keeps rejecting his amorous advances. After all, is he not the Grand Nagus of all the Ferengi?

# A MEMORABLE SUPPORTING CHARACTER
# LI NALAS—
# THE RELUCTANT HERO

*Li Nalas was the focal point of three episodes of Deep Space Nine. He was killed off after his third appearance, unfortunately so because he was one of the most interesting and better developed characters to appear on the series to date.*

What defines a hero? Some say simply being in the right place at the right time and fate will care of the rest. This was never more true than with the legendary Bajoran resistance fighter Li Nalas. Believed slain during a battle with the Cardassians during the occupation, he was actually taken prisoner and kept with other prisoners on a remote asteroid. He remained even after the Cardassians gave the Bajorans their freedom.

No one was more familiar with Li Nalas was than Major Kira. When an informant provided information that Li Nalas was still alive after a decade in a Cardassian prison camp, Kira insisted that she be allowed to go to his aid. She would have done this no matter who was being unjustly imprisoned there; to be told that one of the prisoners was the legendary Li Nalas simply underscored the need to liberate them.

Bajor was having a constitutional crisis. Due to the fate of the religious leader Kai Opaka, and her inability to return to Bajor, the government has become unstable and on the verge of collapse. Li Nalas is exactly the kind of figure around whom the people would rally in this time of crisis, a figure to unite the divisive factions is. One of the factions, The Circle, wanted to sever ties with the Federation and expel all non-Bajorans from the planet. Major Kira knew this would be catastrophic as Bajor was not yet strong enough to stand alone against outside threats, particularly should the Cardassians return.

## The Liberation of a Legend

Major Kira convinces Sisko to support her plan. Chief O'Brien is sent along to assist her, due to his experience in dealing with Cardassians. Their runabout soon finds the prison planet and lands without being detected. They find the camp, which contains only a dozen prisoners. The encampment is surrounded by force fields so they cannot just sneak in or shoot their way in.

Miles O'Brien poses as a pimp and offers Kira's services to the Cardassian guards. They have to see the camp commander first. Once they enter the camp they find Li Nalas, who is amazed to see them. Kira is in awe of Li Nalas as he explains that there are others who must come with them. Li Nalas has lived in the prison camp for ten years and has grown used to the routine. To the Cardassian guards, he is just one more Bajoran prisoner but to his fellow Bajorans, he is a hero. As much as he has resisted, the others have shown him

favor and helped him more than they would have a less illustrious freedom fighter. Li Nalas is troubled by this favoritism but as a prisoner he was willing to take whatever extra measure of comfort he could find. But now he refuses to turn his back on his comrades.

Their plot is discovered before they can free any of the other prisoners. They shoot their way out and Nalas is wounded during the escape. He does not want to leave the other prisoners behind but has no choice. They are outnumbered and if they do not flee, no one will escape. Kira promises to send help for the others. When Cardassian vessels are detected nearing the planet they are forced to escape while they can.

Upon arriving back at Deep Space Nine, Major Kira reports the events at the camp. Inexplicably, Gul Dukat contacts Sisko and states that he was unaware of the prison camp and will immediately free and repatriate the prisoners. Gul Dukat even apologizes for the incident, which is cold comfort for Li Nalas who had been imprisoned for ten years.

## The Pressures of Being a Legend

Li Nalas is healed quickly with Federation technology. Commander Sisko takes him on a tour of Deep Space Nine. Major Kira is clearly impressed whenever she is in the presence of this former leader of the revolution, but Li Nalas seems distracted and uncomfortable, particularly when he is praised by the fellow Bajorans he frequently encounters. Many just assume this is part of his recovery from living cut off from his people for so long and and being forced to endure the lash of his Cardassian captors,. Actually, his feelings go much deeper. Li Nalas believes that he does not deserve this special attention. He loves the freedom, but not the attention; he just wants to be left alone. After all those years in captivity he wants to retire some place in peace and solitude, far from the demands of notoriety. Li Nalas simply wants to find himself again.

Minister Jaro Essa arrives aboard the space station shortly after Li Nalas. Immediately, Jaro starts to curry his favor by playing up to the crowd of Bajorans that have gathered around Nalas. This only makes Nalas uneasy. When Commander Sisko tells Li Nalas that his people need him during this time of crisis on Bajor, Nalas insists that he is the wrong man for the job. Both Sisko and Jaro want Nalas to be a Bajoran leader but that is the furthest thing from the heart and mind of Li Nalas.

In the middle of the night, Li Nalas attempts to stow away on a freighter headed far from Bajor, but he is discovered and turned over to a very surprised Commander Sisko. Why would the hero of Bajor want to flee from the acclaim due him after ten years of captivity? Finally Li Nalas cannot keep the secret any longer and he admits to Ben Sisko the real story of his great heroism.

## The Truth Behind the Legend

His entire reputation is based on accident and exaggeration. He was never a hero. One day while searching for food for his resistance unit, he fell into a lake. Gul Zarale, a much-hated Cardassian officer noted for his brutality, happened to be bathing at the lake. The fact that Zarale was all but naked was probably the only thing that kept Li Nalas alive; in a panic, he shot the Cardassian as the other went for his weapon. The dead Cardassian toppled right on top of Li Nalas. When his companions found him and discovered the identity of the Cardassian he had killed, they made a hero of him. The story of his epic battle with Gul Zarale was quickly elaborated upon until it presented Li Nalas, an ordinary man in an extraordinary situation, as one of the greatest Bajoran freedom fighters of all time.

Li Nalas believed himself to be a fraud, a victim of the need of the Bajoran people to have heroes at a time when they were suffering mightily under the oppression of the Cardassians. Now the war is over and Li Nalas just wants to go off by himself and live his life in peace. By the time he was captured by the Cardassians, Li had resigned himself to serving as a heroic symbol for his people, but he is unwilling to return to that life. He would rather enjoy his freedom far away from the struggle.

Ben Sisko tried to convince Li Nalas that he is still a symbol of freedom, and the Bajoran people need him. Li Nalas fought for his people during the war of attrition against the Cardassians and now he is needed to hold his people together as they war against each other. Reluctantly Li Nalas agrees to try. The Bajoran soon learns that politics is a different kind of warfare. Everyone wanted a piece of him and wanted to use him as an instrument of the future. Some had positive goals and others harbored darker designs.

## The New Bajoran Liaison

To the surprise of many, particularly Commander Sisko and Major Kira, Li Nalas is abruptly appointed Navarch by Minister Jaro. Navarch is a new title created specifically to honor the hero of Bajor, but the position replaces Major Kira as liaison to Deep Space Nine. This is not what Li Nalas wanted and he understands that he is being manipulated by Minister Jaro. Although he had agreed to accept the position, he never agreed to be used by anyone and Jaro soon finds that the "hero of Bajor" is no compliant puppet.

When Kira is rotated back to the surface of Bajor, Li Nalas promises Ben Sisko that he will help to get her restored to the station. Li Nalas will not idly stand by while one of the people who rescued him from the Cardassians is treated so poorly. Jaro made a big mistake: demeaning the person responsible for liberating Li Nalas from prison was unwise.

Commander Sisko suspects that assigning Li Nalas to the station, removing him from Bajor, was done to minimize his influence on the current political situation. Minister Jaro knows that with Li Nalas on the planet, it would only be a matter of time before a splinter group, or perhaps even a coalition, would form around "the hero of Bajor" to support him as the new leader of the government.

Li Nalas is approached by Commander Sisko and asked to learn what he can about the position of the Bajoran military in the current conflict. Li Nalas promises to get to the bottom of what is happening as he accepts the fact that other people have given him authority and respect that he does not feel he has earned. On the other hand, ten years in a Cardassian prison camp should count for something. While Li Nalas does not feel he deserves the acclaim that comes with the "hero of Bajor" sobriquet, as a former prisoner of war he is certainly entitled to respect. He certainly suffered for his people and for his beliefs.

## The Circle Stands Revealed

Quark has learned that the Kressari are supplying weapons to "The Circle," but also, the Kressari are being supplied by the Cardassians. If "The Circle" is being secretly supported by the Cardassians then, as soon as the Federation is kicked off the planet, the Cardassians would take control of the wormhole

Meanwhile, Major Kira has gone to see Vedek Bareil at the monastery. She has a brief encounter with Vedek Winn, who clearly is opposed to what Kira Nerys represents. Shortly after that, Commander Sisko visits Kira and informs her about the Cardassian connection to the "The Circle." As soon as he leaves, Major Kira is kidnapped by masked men. She is taken to the secret hideaway of "The Circle" and encounters its leader—Minister Jaro Essa.

Jaro admits to Kira that Li Nalas was transferred to Deep Space Nine to get him out of the way because

the reluctant hero was a wild card in the minister's carefully laid plans to seize power on Bajor. Jaro himself is "The Circle"; everyone else involved are his henchmen. He needs Kira to reveal the Federation's plans for dealing with the Bajoran situation, but she refuses to divulge any information. Jaro orders that she be tortured.

Quark learns the location of the headquarters of "The Circle." Li Nalas accompanies Chief O'Brien, Dr. Bashir and others on a rescue mission; he has the chance to return the favor to the woman who liberated him from Cardassia IV. The members of the rescue team engage in a fight with Jaro's minions but manage to rescue Kira before she can be badly injured by her torturers.

## The Federation in Exile

Back on the space station they discuss their next move. Li Nalas believes that were he to return to Bajor then he could restore calm. But Commander

Sisko points out that this would also make him a target for assassination. They believe that Li Nalas can help them, but only if he can appeal directly to the Bajoran Chamber of Ministers. In the meantime Minister Jaro has manipulated the Chamber of Ministers into ordering the Federation to leave Bajor by blaming their presence for the unrest. As a result all Federation personnel are ordered to evacuate the space station and leave Bajor.

While most of the personnel prepare to abandon Deep Space Nine, a few elect to remain aboard, securely hidden with the help of the Bajoran Li Nalas. These include Ben Sisko, Chief O'Brien, Dax and Odo. With all of the runabouts taken by the evacuated personnel they need transportation to the surface. Li Nalas tells Kira of the location of some small Bajoran ships hidden on one of the moons of Bajor. Dax and Kira beam over to secure one.

During the evacuation, a crowd of Bajorans (supporters of the Federation) almost riot during the crush to leave the station, but Li Nalas manages to bring calm to the situation by assuring them that all will be well. Li Nalas has learned how his notoriety can be put to good use. Finally the station is evacuated and Li Nalas goes into hiding with the station's command crew. He is at war again but this time against his own people: this is not what he fought for long ago or why he languished in a prison camp for ten years.

## The Hunter

Following the directive issued by the Bajoran Chamber of Ministers, General Krim and his staff arrive to take over Deep Space Nine. The station appears to be abandoned. Jaro's toady, Day Kannu, believes that they won but General Krim is not so sure. Krim believes that Li Nalas and others are still aboard so Day Kannu sends out search parties.. They try to use the sensors in Ops but they have been tampered with so Day's men have to search the station room by room. This was a huge undertaking since Deep Space Nine is capable of holding 7,000 people; Li Nalas and the others had no trouble hiding.

Minister Jaro has anticipated this resistance and he wants Li Nalas taken alive. If Nalas is killed, he will become a Bajoran martyr thus complicating Jaro's plans by giving the opposition a dead hero around whom to rally. However, the search parties find themselves taken prisoner as they encounter Dr. Bashir and others, including Li Nalas. When Colonel Day and his men believe they have captured Li Nalas, Sisko and O'Brien, they discover that instead they have been locked into a holosuite as the images of their prisoners vanish.

Li Nalas has clearly taken sides with the Federation against the Bajoran faction led by Minister Jaro. Li Nalas wants to see his world at peace but not at the price of putting someone like Jaro in power. Bajor needs leaders who care about the greater good of its people. Li Nalas is beginning to believe that he can be of service to his people.

Over the loudspeakers on the space station, Ben Sisko reveals what they have learned about the Cardassian connection and how Jaro has been duped into helping them. Apparently Colonel Day does not believe Sisko. When Day is beamed into Ops and reunited with General Krim, the Colonel does not relay this piece of vital information; Day remains loyal to Jaro. This behavior convinces Li Nalas that he must take his case directly to the Bajoran Chamber of Ministers.

## A Hero at Last

When General Krim's technicians repair the sensors, they immediately locate Sisko and the others. Dr. Bashir distracts them and lures the Bajoran soldiers away from Ops so that Sisko and Li Nalas can return and take over. When General Krim comes back to Ops, Li Nalas tells him that the Cardassians are behind "The Circle." General Krim is as impressed with Li Nalas as are many other Bajorans and so he listens to what he is told. Krim returns command of the space station to Ben Sisko.

The traitorous Colonel Day will not accept Krim's decision and he draws his weapon intending to slay Sisko on the spot. Li Nalas heroically tries to stop Colonel Day and is mortally wounded. As Dr. Bashir valiantly but unsuccessfully tries to save the Bajoran's life, Li Nalas looks at Sisko and remarks, "Off the hook," knowing that he will no longer have to live up to anyone's unrealistic expectations of him nor bear the responsibility that comes with being a living legend. The hero of Bajor has fulfilled the destiny Minister Jaro tried to prevent and has become a martyr.

However Li Nalas may have regarded himself, he was truly a hero. He died a hero's death by working for the good of the people of Bajor. With the death of Li Nalas, and the truth about the Cardassian conspiracy revealed, order comes to Bajor. Minister Jaro and Vedek Winn find their plans in a shambles, yet they live to plot another day, while Li Nalas, the man who just wanted to put the war behind him, has fallen victim to his fellow Bajorans. Politics twisted and reshaped the life of Li Nalas after he was freed from the Cardassian prison camp. When he returned to Bajor he found not only an unexpected hero's homecoming but treachery at the hands of some of his own people—treachery that ultimately led to his death. What could Li Nalas have accomplished had he lived? He was only starting to come to terms with this question when he was cruelly struck down.

# A MEMORABLE VILLAIN
# GUL DUKAT

*Before Ben Sisko, Jadzia Dax and the other members of Deep Space Nine, there was Gul Dukat. Gul Dukat was the former Cardassian Prefect of the space station and occupied the very office now used by Commander Sisko. Unlike other Cardassians who have come and gone, Gul Dukat has been a recurring presence in the series over the past two years, beginning with the very first one, "Emissary." Perhaps his most interesting appearance was as the menacing presence running the space station in the flashback sequences in the episode "Necessary Evil."*

Gul Dukat was the Cardassian Prefect on the mining station orbiting Bajor and he enjoyed his position of power over the Bajorans. His homeworld of Cardassia was an empire builder and, decades before, they had annexed Bajor along that road to empire. Dukat took full advantage of the respect and fear that came with being a member of the conquering race.

Dukat joined the military and demonstrated all of the ruthless qualities that insured rapid advancement. When he was posted to Bajor as the military Prefect on the mining station, he found himself confronted with surly Bajorans and a rampant underground network of terrorism that he vowed to crush, so long as his executions did not interfere too much with the available labor pool. When of his Bajoran collaborators, Vetrik, was murdered Dukat found himself in a difficult situation. Were he or any other Cardassian to become directly involved in the investigation of the murder it would draw undue attention to the crime. The Cardassians believed in protecting their collaborators but to put too much emphasis on this one Bajoran's death would arouse suspicion. The Bajorans would look more carefully at this man's associates—associates on whom Gul Dukat was depending for information on underground activities.

## MAINTAINING CONTROL

A neutral third party was required. Dukat appointed Odo, the shape-shifter, an alien with no past who was neither Bajoran nor Cardassian and expressed no allegiance to either side. At first, the shape-shifter resisted acting as a Cardassian agent. Gul Dukat is clever, though, and without revealing the truth of the situation he explained that unless there is some sort of official investigation then the Cardassian High Command will order him to execute ten Bajorans at random as an object lesson and an exercise in civilian control. Odo reluctantly agreed investigate in order to help maintain order among the Bajorans living on the space station.

While Gul Dukat believed that the shape-shifter is a good choice for dealing with the captive population, the Cardassian is eager to find the culprit. Did someone know that Vetrik was a collaborator or was the man's death just a random murder committed when someone was caught burglarizing the man's shop? Gul Dukat found Odo interrogating a Bajoran woman named Kira Nerys. Could she be the one? His information on her indicated that she was a low level operative in the Bajoran underground—little more than a courier. Could she be a threat? He supposed that he could have her executed on general principles; but if he began killing everyone with ties to the underground, however innocuous, then they would have few left for the menial labor the Cardassians require.

When Gul Dukat entered Odo's office, Kira was just being released. He asked Odo if she was a suspect in the crime: Odo stated categorically that she was not a suspect. Dukat regretfully let her pass from the office into the Promenade as he was so hoping that she might have been the murderer. Having one's collaborators killed creates such undue hardship on the ruling class.

## THE END OF AN ERA

Odo kept investigating the crime but he was never able to find the perpetrator. By then there were other criminal matters to look into and the murder of Vetrik faded into the background. After all, what is the death of one Bajoran on a world the size of Bajor? Utlimately Gul Dukat had to agree because as Prefect he could not show undue interest in what seemed to be simply another random killing. Reluctantly he had to accept that the murder would go unsolved and be satisfied that he still had access to Vetrik's cronies who could pick up where Vetrik had left off.

Gul Dukat remained in close contact with Odo for the next five years and even played Kalevian Montar with the shape-shifter once. He cheated when he played but Gul Dukat considered cheating a legitimate part of any game.

When it came time for the Cardassians to pull out from Bajor after decades of occupation, Gul Dukat opposed the move. Kotan Pedar and the civilian authorities countermanded his opposition because Bajor no longer had anything to offer Cardassia. The planet had been stripped of its mineral wealth and it certainly had no strategic advantage. Gul Dukat, however, believed that there were other uses for the planet and one did not play the game of empire by relinquishing a conquered world. His protests went unheeded and he vowed to one day get back at Kotan Pedar for robbing him of this position of power. He believed that leaving Bajor could be turned to his advantage due to an intrigue, regarding Koran, that he had put into motion. Time would tell.

## THE BAJORAN WORM-HOLE

Because the Cardassians willingly left Bajor they felt no compunction about visiting the space station. Soon after Ben Sisko was posted at Deep Space Nine, he heard from the former Prefect, Gul

Dukat. Dukat and his aides arrived shortly after the Enterprise left the space station, as though they were uncomfortable with visiting while the power of the Enterprise was too close at hand. Dukat visited Sisko in the commander's office and the Cardassian fished for information about the orb. Gul Dukat had reliable intelligence information; the Cardassian knew about the orbs and the fact that they signify great power. However, while the Cardassians were in charge on Bajor the religious leaders were hidden and would share little or nothing with their alien overlords. When Dukat inquired about the orbs Sisko replied that he knew nothing about them, which was the truth at that time. Gul Dukat was unhappy with Sisko's non-responsiveness and implied that Cardassia has by no means forgotten about Bajor, particularly if it proves to have more of value to offer. Dukat's ship remained docked at the station while his men visited the Promenade.

Later Sisko and Dax were in a runabout when they encountered a wormhole—what turned out to be the first stable wormhole in the known galaxy. After Dax suggested that the wormhole may well be artificial, which accounts for its stability, Gul Dukat's vessel moved away from the space station in order to investigate this fantastic phenomenon.

After Sisko and Dax entered the wormhole, Major Kira and O'Brien devised a way of safely extending the orbit of Deep Space Nine to place it closer to the wormhole and thereby stake a claim on it for Bajor. When Major Kira tried to warn Gul Dukat's ship that the wormhole might not be safe to enter, the Cardassian played dumb, claiming to know nothing about any wormhole. In this way he could "accidentally" discover it for Cardassia. His ship entered it and vanished from the Alpha Quadrant. The wormhole then vanished as miraculously as it appeared.

## GUL DUKAT—LOST IN SPACE?

Gul Dukat had sent word to a Cardassian fleet: they approached Bajor only to learn that Gul Dukat had vanished. They demanded that he be returned and accused Major Kira of disposing of the former Prefect of Bajor. She denied this but neither could she produce evidence of Gul Dukat's whereabouts. She could not prove that Gul Dukat was alive and if the wormhole did not reappear, the Cardassian vessel would take seventy years to return to the Alpha Quadrant from the Gamma Quadrant. If Kira could not produce concrete answers soon then the Cardassians would attack Deep Space Nine.

Inside the wormhole, the "Prophets," the non-humanoid aliens who created the wormhole, determined they could trust Sisko and his species. Luckily they also understood that the Cardassians are not representative of the humanoid races in the galaxy. They agree to allow Gul Dukat's ship to return through the wormhole. Just as the Cardassian fleet was about to attack the space station, the wormhole opened and a runabout emerged towing Gul Dukat's vessel on a tractor beam. With Gul Dukat returned safely the Cardassians had no reason to attack and they reluctantly withdrew.

Gul Dukat wished there was some way they could have taken back Bajor and Deep Space Nine and thereby control the miraculous opportunities this wormhole offered. He knows, however, that they cannot declare war on Bajor so long as the Federation is aligned with them. He can hope for the future, though, and so he maintains a dialogue with the space station.

## A QUESTION OF CARDASSIAN GUILT

When a Cardassian arrives on the space station, suspected of being the war criminal Gul Darhe'el, Gul Dukat assures them that he is Aamin Marritza, a military file clerk. Initially Dukat is angry because a Cardassian is being detained and demands that Sisko release him. As the situation drags on Gul Dukat realizes that there was more than meets the eye: the Bajorans are not trying to stir up trouble but this lone Cardassian citizen is.

Odo investigates the matter and because of his previous association with Gul Dukat, the Cardassian co-operates with Odo's investigation. Gul Dukat has no interest in seeing Cardassia smeared by the Federation and he knows any lies he tells will eventually backfire; so he tells the truth. Gul Darhe'el, the notorious "Butcher of Gallitepp" (as he is known on Bajor) has been dead for five years. The mysterious Cardassian aboard Deep Space Nine is deliberately masquerading as Gul Darhe'el for some unknown purposes.

Apparently Marritza was a clerk at Gallitepp and witnessed the atrocities there, war crimes for which Cardassia has never answered. Marritza felt guilty because he was too cowardly to stand up to his superiors, and decry their criminal behavior. This guilt was manifested in the desire to stand trial himself for the crimes of Gul Darhe'el and thereby draw attention to what Cardassia has successfully ignored. When Marritza is exposed, he is slain by one of the survivors of Gallitepp, insuring that he will not return to Cardassia and drum up support for a war crimes tribunal. For Gul Dukat, in war there are no crimes—just winners and losers. After all, Bajoran terrorists were certainly responsible for the deaths of innocent Cardassian civilians and no one called those war crimes.

## THE KRESSARI CONNECTION

Gul Dukat knows that the Cardassians had other dirty little secrets. One of these secrets is a prison camp on Cardassia IV where Bajorans were still being held although the Cardassians had freed

Bajor from their domination. When Dukat learns that Major Kira and Miles O'Brien have liberated one of these prisoners he immediately frees the others and repatriates them to Bajor. His intentions for doing so are by no means benevolent. He is simply trying to maintain the pose Cardassia has adopted for the Federation: that they no longer have any interest in the world of Bajor or its political future. In truth, the leaders of Cardassia still chaff over the fact that they gave up Bajor right before it became one of the most important junctures of commerce in the galaxy. They refuse to forget about what they have lost.

A Bajoran faction exists who resent the intrusion of any non-Bajorans (thanks, of course, to their memories of decades under the heel of Gul Dukat and his predecessors). The Cardassians use a middle man, in the form of the alien race known as the Kressari, to supply weapons to this faction. In this way they succeed in creating a confrontation which will lead to the

Federation being expelled from Bajor. The Bajorans do not realize, however, that as soon as the Federation leaves, the Cardassians will move back in. Since the Bajorans would have dissolved their alignment with the Federation, they would be defenseless. Much to Gul Dukat's chagrin, the Cardassian connection to the underground group called "The Circle" is exposed, effectively destroying the anti-Federation faction. It was close, but Gul Dukat had to watch this delicately wrought Cardassian plot crash and burn.

But there is always the next time.

## THE CASE OF THE CARDASSIAN ORPHAN

Sometimes there are plots which have nothing to do with Bajoran domination but instead have to do with Cardassian internecine warfare; such is the case of Cardassian war orphans. Because Cardassians place no value on orphans, their neglect seemed to be a function of the culture.

A Cardassian boy named Rugel was being raised by Bajorans and there were suspicions that Rugel was being abused. While the Cardassians seem uninterested in the situation, Sisko and others are concerned, including a Cardassian named Garak. When Garak tries to talk to the boy, Rugal attack Garak. This attack brings up the question of whether the boy is being taught to hate all Cardassians, although he is a Cardassian. After the attack, Garak reveals he believes the orphans were left behind intentionally, citing that fact that the Cardassians do not make mistakes of that sort. Cardassians are renowned for their attention to detail.

## DUKAT IS CROSS-EXAMINED

Gul Dukat, seemingly concerned about the status of the boy, contacts Commander Sisko and asks for a sample of the boy's DNA so that they can find any existing relatives on Cardassia. Sisko agreed and Gul Dukat is pleased. In the middle of their conversation Dr. Bashir, who has been getting an earful from Garak, questions Gul Dukat's involvement, particularly since Dukat supervised the withdrawal from Bajor. Bashir wonders how the Cardassian orphans were overlooked. Gul Dukat diverts the question by explaining that the civilian Cardassian leaders—not the military, of which he is a part—made the decision to withdraw. He regrets that the civilian leaders decided to leave the Cardassian children behind. Sisko and the others find it difficult to imagine Gul Dukat expressing regret or any gentle emotions; the Cardassian military has never expressed regret for anything, except for leaving Bajor too soon.

Garak is an old adversary of Gul Dukat's but their connection remains murky. Clearly they crossed paths at some point. Garak has been waiting for the chance to repay Gul Dukat for some past offense: now, repayment can be accomplished simply by revealing the truth.

Meanwhile, Gul Dukat contacted Sisko to reveal that Rugal's father has been discovered. He is Kotan Pedar, a prominent Cardassian politician who was in the civilian command on Bajor at the time of the pull out of forces. Pedar thought that the boy was killed in a terrorist attack on Bajor, in which Rugal's mother was slain.

## PLOT AND COUNTER-PLOT

Garak believes there is more to the story than meets the eye. He takes Dr. Bashir down to the orphanage on Bajor from where Rugal was adopted. Garak reveals that Kotan Pedar was actually the civilian leader responsible for the evacuation of Bajor, a move Gul Dukat opposed. He remains a political enemy of Gul Dukat. While orphans have no status on Cardassia, families do. If it is revealed that Kotan

Pedar abandoned his son on Bajor to be raised by Bajorans, he will be disgraced—unless Garak and Dr. Bashir can unearth the truth.

Things seem to go in Gul Dukat's favor: when Kotan Pedar arrives to reclaim his son, not only does the boy reject him, he condemns all Cardassians. He is not even moved when told that his mother died in the same attack in which Kotan believed that Rugal had been killed. A custody hearing is held on Deep Space Nine. Sisko is surprised that Gul Dukat arrives to observe. Dukat perhaps overplayed his hand by showing up in person. He claims he was there out of concern for the Cardassian war orphans, an issue he had expressed no official interest in before.

## GUL DUKAT EXPOSED

Garak discovered that Rugal was not found by Bajorans as had been believed. He was actually brought to the orphanage several years before the evacuation by a Cardassian military officer attached to the command post at Terak Nor. The question is raised that if Rugal was left at the orphanage by a military officer, was it part of a plot to one day ruin the reputation of Kotan Pedar? Gul Dukat was the commanding officer who ordered that Rugal be brought to the orphanage; he determined that eight years later he would be able to engineer the downfall of Kotan Pedar by revealing the existence of the man's long lost son.

Because Sisko knows the truth, Gul Dukat agrees not to publicize Kotan Pedar's personal problems. Rugal is returned to his father. This annoys Gul Dukat but should it be proven that he kidnapped Kotan's child and abandoned him in a Bajoran orphanage, Gul Dukat would be humiliated and disgraced. Gul Dukat does not like his plots being undermined. He longs for the days when he was still in charge of the space station, when his word was law and he could consign people to their deaths.

After all, he has trained his whole life for this power and believes that Cardassians are a superior breed, that it is their birthright to exercise their superiority over lesser races.

Dukat hopes that those days will return. Gul Dukat and the Cardassian High Command are now in full agreement on the mistake the civilian authorities made in abandoning Bajor, now a vital link in the chain of galactic commerce. While Cardassia is allowed to use the wormhole, they are not satisfied to simply use it, they want to control it. Gul Dukat would be at the head of any such force if Cardassia regains power on Bajor.

# THE WRAP-UP

# A LOOK AT THE DEEP SPACE CREW:
# A NEW CORNER OF THE
# Star Trek UNIVERSE

Deep Space Nine marks the first Star Trek series to be created without the guiding hand of Gene Roddenberry. But is this good or bad? While on the original Star Trek, the characters argued from time to time and were by no means perfect, they always did the right thing in the end. On Star Trek—The Next Generation the main characters never argued among themselves, and only occasionally with outsiders. But what about DEEP SPACE NINE? These are not all Federation enlistees: Major Kira was drafted out of the Bajoran resistance, Odo is a holdover from the Cardassian regime which ran the station, and Quark—well Quark is a Ferengi and their only allegiance is to gold press latinum. These are characters unlike what one would normally expect to find on the bridge of the starship Enterprise.

And of course this is not the Enterprise. Rather, it is a former Cardassian mining station on orbit around Bajor, a backwater world until the discovery of the only stable wormhole made it a hub of commerce in that part of the galaxy. With it comes the colorful characters one would expect to find in these extraordinary circumstances. How interesting are they and how do they compare with their counterparts on the starships we have come to know so well?

## The Commander Benjamin Sisko

Ben Sisko comes out of Starfleet, the home of two other well known career officers, Captain Jean-Luc Picard and Captain James T. Kirk. Like them, Sisko has suffered both victory and defeat; but unlike them, Sisko has a family and lost his wife in the battle with the Borg at Wolf 359. While Picard is more likely to consult with his staff before making a decision, Commander Sisko tells his staff what his decision is and how it can best be implemented. The pressure is on him to deliver and deliver he does.

Picard has been forbidden to lead away teams and Kirk was the officer responsible for that directive. However, Ben Sisko has no problem leaving Deep Space Nine and leading a mission into the wormhole. He led one such journey at Kai Opaka's request. In this episode, Sisko soon found himself in trouble and reconsidered the wisdom of his decision to lead the mission. After all, he not only has responsibilities to the space station but also to his son.

Although Sisko has a central office on Deep Space Nine in Ops (Operations), he likes to walk through the station, observing the bustle of activity and looking out at the stars. He has occasionally used one of the station's runabouts to go through the wormhole and visit the Gamma Quadrant, his is not a mission of exploration and discover as was the captains of the Enterprise; Sisko's is a mission of diplomacy.

Sisko was first assigned to deal with the newly independent world of Bajor which was requesting admission to the Federation and aid rebuilding from the destructive occupation of the Cardassians. But now Sisko acts as ambassador to races who come through the wormhole from the Gamma Quadrant and who have never had contact with the Federation.

The career Ben Sisko chose is proving to be filled with surprises. He does not always feel that it is the ideal place to raise a son, but Jake has has learned to appreciate what each new place has to offer. Ben Sisko has done the same. Like Picard and Kirk before him, Sisko has many lives depending on the wisdom of his decisions.

## The First Officer
## Major Kira Nerys

Major Kira is in illustrious company with the title of first officer. Commander William Riker of the Enterprise-D holds this title, and years before, that by Commander Spock of the legendary first starship Enterprise was first officer. Unlike the other first officers, Kira's background is as a freedom fighter and terrorist, not as a Starfleet cadet who graduated at the top of their class. While Spock and Riker became fast friends with their commanding officers, Major Kira had a rocky start. She initially resented Commander Sisko's presence. They have found that they have more in com-

mon than not but they still disagree, particularly on issues relating to Bajor. Kira is very devoted to the religion of her planet and stands by a religious leader, although she is also willing to realize when her faith has been used to manipulate her. She also confronts Commander Sisko in matters of policy relating to the Cardassians. She hates the Cardassians for what they did to her people and her world. Kira has learned, though, that not all Cardassians are alike.

Kira soon came to recognize that the Federation was not a threat to Bajor. In fact, she even withstood torture rather than reveal how the Federation planned to project the Bajoran government from the revolt engineered by Minister Jaro. She found that she had true friends on Deep Space Nine when Sisko and Quark teamed up to rescue her. Kira understands that Commander Sisko regards her as more than just his liaison to Bajor.

## Security Officer
## Constable Odo

No security officer on the Enterprise—not even Worf—has been anything like Security Chief Odo. Although an alien, as is Worf, Odo is from a non-humanoid race and is capable of turning any object, animate or inanimate. Unlike his earlier counterparts, he does not know his origins. Odo is, in some ways, a reflection of the Bajorans who found and raised him. Dr. Mora was a father figure to Odo but studied Odo as much as he raised him. Like any son, Odo left his home to find his place in the world: he found his place in the law. Odo has no training in law enforcement but has an innate sense of justice. The ability to change his form makes him the ideal detective.

Although Odo never knew his predecessors, Worf and Tasha Yar, they also grew up far from their own kind. Yar left the planet of her birth as soon as she could. Worf returns to his planet whenever possible, in an attempt to discover his own culture. Worf and Odo have much in common: Worf was raised by humans far from his people just as Odo was raised by Bajorans far from his unknown homeworld. Worf, however, accepts his foster parents and makes them a part of his existence; Odo has rejected his foster father, although he has made a rapprochement with him recently.

Of the three security officers, Odo is the least likely to use weapons. In fact his security system detects weapons so that they will not be carried onto the Promenade. Of course, Odo does not need to carry a weapon: he has built-in protection in his ability to reshape his body, a system any security officer would envy.

## SCIENCE OFFICER
## Jadzia Dax

The duty of science officer has a tendency to fall on non-humans: Data, the android; Spock, the Vulcan; and now Lt. Jadzia Dax, the Trill. Perhaps their otherworldly qualities allow them to excel in this position. Dax more similar to Data than she is to Spock. Although Vulcans can live to be 200 years, Trills can live for many hundreds of years because they are transferred into another body when their host form dies. Data has an artificial body which could last thousands of year. While Data is more machine than man, Dax is a humanoid capable of emotions. The ability to feel has allowed her to better enjoy her life and her duties. Her long life has enabled her to attain an expertise working with computers; she could easily work alongside Data and Spock.

## MEDICAL OFFICER
### Lieutenant Julian Bashire

Dr. Julian Bashir is something new in the Star Trek universe. Unlike the veterans we have seen previously—Beverly Crusher, Katherine Pulaski and Leonard McCoy—Julian is at the beginning of his career. His only experience is his schooling at Starfleet Medical but he is no doubt as intelligent and prepared as were the other physicians when they tackled the demands of space medicine years. A recent graduate of the Starfleet Medical Academy, at 26 he is both sharp and eager. He requested a deep space posting because he knew could gain invaluable experience. In twenty years Dr. Bashir will doubtless be just as well known, highly respected and in demand as Leonard McCoy and Dr. Crusher.

Space has great need for physicians like Dr. Bashir. He specializes in xenobiology— the study of alien species. Like his predecessors he has not forgotten the the importance of dealing with a patient as an individual, even when it is a non-human. Unlike Crusher, McCoy and others, Dr. Bashir found himself dropped into a medlab on Deep Space Nine which had been thoroughly trashed. He needed all of his knowledge and skills to rebuild the medical facility into one capable of dealing with any medical emergency.

## CHIEF ENGINEER
### Chief Miles O'Brien

Miles O'Brien was a whiz with the transporters when he was stationed on the Enterprise-D, but once aboard Deep Space Nine he discovered skills he did not even know he had. He got a crash course in what it must be like to be Lt. Commander Montgomery Scott, the legendary Enterprise engineer. Scotty could solve almost any problem in his engine room and, similarly, Miles O'Brien has learned how to solve almost any mechanical problem.

If Scotty was considered to be a miracle-worker for pulling off feats such as wiring Romulan technology so that it would operate on a Federation starship (in the case of the stolen cloaking device), then Miles O'Brien has accomplished similar wonders. He repaired the mechanical devices ruined by the departing Cardassians. He even was able to fool the Cardassian sensors into thinking that the station was fully armed with photon torpedoes. At the same time, he held station together with a force field while they moved into a different orbit, closer to the Bajoran wormhole.

O'Brien brings many years of experience with him. He spent five years on the Enterprise and, before that, he spent seventeen years on other vessels and postings. While O'Brien had specific duties in his previous postings, on Deep Space Nine he is in charge of everything. His title, Chief of Operations, is as demanding as it implies. Unlike the Enterprise and the Federation ships he was on, the equipment on Deep Space Nine is not the latest technology nor is it being updated during stopovers at starbases.

O'Brien's twenty-three years in Starfleet have prepared him for his role as trouble-shooter on Deep Space Nine, a role in which he must be both Geordi LaForge and Montgomery Scott.

## Your Host for the Evening...
## Quark

Quark is the opposite of Guinan. Guinan is friendly and helpful; Quark is genial only when you are spending money on drinks and losing money at the Dabo tables. And then there's the matter of the kinky holosuite programs...programs that are probably not readily accessible on the Enterprise.

Whatever human perfection there may be in the 24th century, it has nothing to do with the Ferengi. They have their own code of existence called the "Rules of Acquisition"; they live to acquire. Whereas Guinan wants her customers in Ten Forward to relax and enjoy themselves, Quark wants his customers in "Quark's Place" to relax and enjoy spending their money. When Kira talks him into allowing a talented out of work Bajoran minstrel to play in the bar, Quark becomes irate that his customers stop buying and instead listen to the music. He calculates his profits by the hour, and for two hours his profits went down. He finally compromised so long as the musician played something more "bouncy" and exciting rather than slow and melancholy. While Guinan is willing to listen to someone's problems, Quark is more interested in hearing some juicy tidbit of information which he can use later. Quark is unlike Guinan in another way: she has many friends. Quark is only tolerated by a few people and he has many enemies.

Such is life on Deep Space Nine, a part of the galaxy where a wild cross-section of people are found, representing every element of the known (and possibly the unknown) universe.

# ORDER FORM

# 100% Satisfaction Guaranteed.

We value your support. You will receive a full refund as long as the copy of the book you are not happy with is received back by us in reasonable condition. No questions asked, except we would like to know how we failed you. Refunds and credits are given as soon as we receive back the item you do not want.

NAME:_____

STREET:_____

CITY:_____

STATE:_____

ZIP:_____

TOTAL:_____ SHIPPING_____

SEND TO: Couch Potato, Inc. 5715 N. Balsam Rd., Las Vegas, NV 89130